azorno

WITHDRAWN
UTSA LIBRARIES

D0771858

ALSO BY INGER CHRISTENSEN

Available from New Directions

alphabet

Butterfly Valley

It

inger christensen

a z o r n o

TRANSLATED FROM THE DANISH
BY DENISE NEWMAN

a new directions book

Copyright © 1967, 1984, 2005 by Inger Christensen and Gyldendal
Translation copyright © 2009 by Denise Newman

All rights reserved. Except for brief passages quoted in a newspaper, magazine,
radio, or television review, no part of this book may be reproduced in any form or
by any means, electronic or mechanical, including photocopying and recording,
or by any information storage and retrieval system, without permission in writing
from the Publisher.

This publication received the support of the
Literature Committee of the Danish Arts Council.

The translator wishes to thank Susanna Nied, Bjarne Funch, Michael Pedersen,
and Eléna Rivera for their invaluable help with this translation,
and Declan Spring for his astute editing.

Quotation by Søren Kierkegaard from: *Either/Or*. Part I.
Edited and translated by Howard V. Hong and Edna H. Hong
(Princeton: Princeton Univ. Press, 1987) p. 92.

Book design by Sylvia Frezzolini Severance
Manufactured in the United States of America
New Directions Books are printed on acid-free paper.
First published by New Directions as New Directions Paperbook NDP1138 in 2009
Published simultaneously in Canada by Penguin Books Canada Limited

Library of Congress Cataloging-in-Publication Data

Christensen, Inger, 1935–2009.
[Azorno. English]
Azorno / Inger Christensen ; translated from the Danish
by Denise Newman.
p. cm.
ISBN 978-0-8112-1657-9 (alk. paper)
1. Authors—Fiction. 2. Fictitious characters—Fiction.
3. Experimental fiction. I. Newman, Denise. II. Title.
PT8176.13.H727A913 2009
839.81'374—dc22   2009016786

Library
University of Texas
at San Antonio

New Directions Books are published for James Laughlin
by New Directions Publishing Corporation
80 Eighth Avenue, New York, NY 10011

Human Beings, as I see them, are

 1. created by form

 2. creators of form,

 its tireless executors.

    —WITOLD GOMBROWICZ

I've learned that I'm the woman he first meets on page eight.

It was Azorno who told me. Come to think of it, I've never dared to ask him why he's called Azorno.

We were supposed to meet just to the right of the main entrance, under those big trees, where people wait so they won't get in anyone's way. I was wearing a white hat, and when I passed through the turnstile everything fell completely silent.

The man waiting for me wasn't Azorno.

Within a second my blood, my thoughts, nerves, and senses were swept back ten years and I think I felt like a diver who finds himself at the bottom of the ocean one minute and on solid ground the next, unable to hear whether the others are saying he's dead or alive because he's encapsulated in a silence as vast as if he'd brought the ocean up with him and it surrounded him now like a huge bell that no one could pass through without drowning.

The next second was very painful, or rather I felt it as pain. I wanted to avoid meeting the past, and so I turned quickly and tried to leave the way I'd entered, through the turnstile, but of course it turns only one way. Azorno came whirling through, grabbed me, and swung me around, laughing. Then we walked on into the gardens with our arms around each other.

And I saw that there was no longer anyone standing under the big trees whose shadows peacefully slid over and past us, while Azorno spoke about the imagery of certain artists, about water and water lilies, parasols and white clouds and fabrics, a wealth of the kind of luminous, tangible things that are supposed to evoke the intangible, and which now suddenly had assembled in one specific place in the world, resting around me like a bell, Azorno said, a silence.

By this time we had come to the wide tulip beds. Do you know Azorno? I can't recall if I've seen you together, but of course you could have met each other in places I don't go.

All the tulips were the same pale green, but the groupings had faint suggestions of other colors as well, and I understood that they would bloom in a specific pattern according to the vision of the gardener, a vision he must have had one cold winter's day when Tivoli was covered with snow.

While I chatted about the flowers, the weather, and the long winter, Azorno had begun, without my noticing, to tell me about Sampel's new novel. I calmly continued to speak about the way the tulips were growing, for no one, not even Azorno, can conceal the fact that retellings of novels seem like gossip about other people's private lives. Anyway, the book is supposed to be excellent. Have you ever read Sampel?

I think I'd been telling him about a bouquet of multi-colored tulips that Katarina once gave me, when suddenly we both fell silent, and we kept walking down past the lake and all the way around it until we came back to the tulip beds, where we sat down at a table and ordered two Dubonnets.

I was a little sorry that we hadn't spoken about the lake. It was the same pale green as the tulips, but it wasn't from the reflection of the trees since they hadn't come into leaf yet, and it wasn't from the sky either, since of course that was blue.

Azorno started talking about Sampel's novel again, and eventually I realized he was serious, because he took my hand, and while he was playing with it a little awkwardly, maybe with a slightly studied awkwardness, he slowly revealed to me that he had wanted to meet me here to tell me that a couple of days ago he learned I was the woman whom the main character in Sampel's novel first meets on page eight.

*

After reading these two typewritten pages, I had to slide them back quickly under the many papers spread over the writing desk, which were all, whether written on or not, lying blank side up. I heard footsteps in the long, tiled gallery, heard Randi scold the dog in German, and heard with increasing clarity the squeaking casters under the heavy tea cart, which was so heavy that it really needed two people to push it from the kitchen down through the gallery to the different rooms. Still, Randi used it every day.

I opened the door and right away the dog began chewing on the raised threshold. Randi gave the dog, Goethe, a cookie, and he immediately ran in and sat in the big blue armchair.

I understood that this was a trick that they enjoyed, and I smiled.

So this was the sunroom I'd heard so much about.

This was where Randi had tea every afternoon with Goethe, or with Goethe and others, as today with Goethe and me, or perhaps the other day, or last year, with Goethe and Azorno.

All the way down through Germany I'd been longing for this sunroom that I'd heard so much about.

It proved to remarkably meet my expectations: Sure

enough there were seven very tall windows, three along the south wall that stretched the width of the house, with, by the way, Lake Zurich immersed in the landscape far below; two to the west, overlooking lower-lying houses with their parks, gardens, groves, and small ponds or pools; and one to the east, with an unobstructed view of blue mountains floating in the distance.

I had now firmly resolved to find out the truth about the letter or that part of the letter that I'd just read and which we now turned our backs on while we had tea.

Finally there was a window to the north, since the house was a little wider here in the corner where the gallery met the sunroom, this sunroom that I'd heard so much about, first and foremost because of this window to the north.

Because of its design, this room could catch the sunlight from the earliest to the latest hours, even on the longest and lightest summer day.

It had rained all the way down through Germany and was still raining. The windows to the north and west were nearly black with rain, and those to the south and east grew steadily grayer with rain.

Even so, the sunroom shone with such a radiance that all my longing was dissolved into a perfect calm.

I have to mention right away that the darkest spot in the room was the blue armchair with Goethe, but this was also the only dark spot. Everything else was altogether dazzling, and if there was any color, it was the same color as tulip beds before they come into bloom, a pale green. By the way, I think the furniture was made of ivory. But of course it might have just been painted white.

These observations may seem superficial, like a set of

parentheses in the previously mentioned perfect calm, which I still must have looked as if I were enjoying, but at the same time, they may also be understood as a kind of deep and irritating annoyance, like an itch, arising precisely in response to the very perfection of the calm.

When I looked at Goethe I had to admit he was smiling.

And how that dog could smile!

In fact, it may not even have been the sunroom that was having such a strong effect. That effect was certainly something we had all experienced before and in very different places. And that's why this dog in the blue armchair could sit there boldly sharing his anxious awareness that a perfect calm is always a painful silence.

—The sunroom always makes a strong impression on everyone, Randi said. The dog barked and I took a cookie, and—managed to say that I had read the letter.

—As we always did in the old days, I added, smiling, while the rain buzzed in my ears.

—What letter?

—Well, that's what I wanted to ask. Who is the letter from, or are you in the middle of writing it?

Randi had stood up.

—It's about Azorno, I said.

Randi leafed through the papers on the writing desk.

—I didn't write it, she said then.

—I know Azorno very well, I said.

—Possibly in the same way that I know Sampel, said Randi.

Goethe barked. Randi gave him a cookie, and he jumped onto my lap and stretched his muzzle down the length of my thighs. I settled beneath him and looked welcoming.

Actually, it didn't matter which one of us knew Azorno

and which one of us knew Sampel. But of course it would be very interesting if the letter were from the author himself, since then it would be all about an author's close relationship with his two main characters.

—It's from Xenia.

Randi let the letter slide back among the many sheets of paper that were spread over the writing desk.

—I don't think I know her.

And then Randi told me all about Xenia.

It grew into a very long and actually a very sad story, which I'm completely incapable of retelling, mainly because I object to Randi's way of presenting it. She didn't speak about Xenia, but about Xenia's character.

The sunset had ended somewhere far beyond the rain and mountains, and the sunroom appeared more and more radiant. By the way, I don't think Randi was even trying to get close to the truth, if for a moment I consider the truth to be the actual circumstances.

At the end of the story was the frightening revelation that the story itself was precisely the reason for my being asked to drive as quickly as possible down through Germany, because Randi, on account of this whole story, etc., needed me, etc., etc.

—What do you mean? I asked.

—Well, said Randi, I wanted to ask you to rescue Xenia.

—What do you mean? I said, sounding more foolish than before.

—Well, Randi said, you have to help her understand that she's caught in a daydream.

—How could that be? I said helplessly.

—Well, said Randi, you must explain everything to her,

tell her that I was with Sampel the other day, and that he told me *I'm* the woman whom the main character in his novel first meets on page eight.

What do you mean? I almost said, but stopped myself.

—And do you know who the main character is, the man? continued Randi. It's Azorno, and Sampel wants to introduce me to Azorno, on the first Sunday in May. She smiled. Goethe barked and ran anxiously back and forth in front of the door to the gallery.

—But what, I asked, do you want me to do?

—Anything, tell her something or other, be with her, entertain her, something, anything . . . Want to come along while I take the dog downstairs?

I stood up and went over to Randi and she put her arm around my shoulders and we walked through the gallery.

—You know what I mean, she said. I just want you to keep her away from both Sampel and Azorno, at least keep her away from them until I've had enough time with Azorno to get an impression of him.

We went down the wide stone staircase at the center of the house, and I could hear Goethe scratching at some door down there; it turned out to be a door leading from the inner courtyard out to the garden. Randi opened the door, the rain blew in for a moment, and we sat down on the stone bench in the colonnade. Outside, a fountain splashed in the garden with a tone other than rain.

—She's always been quite a liar, Randi said.

Goethe rushed in with a bone, shook off the rain, and started chewing on it. I was picking at an old sandstone sculpture, a little greenish manikin with oversized ears and waves down the chest as on a washboard to signify frizzy hair.

—Xenia's always been quite a liar, Randi said.

I promised to do what I could, mostly because I couldn't stand thinking how meaningless my whole trip down through Germany would've been otherwise, with all my longing to see the sunroom that I'd heard so much about, and then having it rain the whole time.

So I promised to do what I could, and we went upstairs again and she kindly and absently showed me the many carved wooden chests along the walls of the gallery. She didn't open any of them, and we didn't go back to the sunroom.

I didn't ask her about anything specific. She said she'd bought the big bouquets of flowers the day before.

I glanced at a couple of the many photographs and paintings that hung on the walls.

Randi said that each one had a story.

Then we took a quick tour through some of the many carefully furnished rooms, all unusable because of their deadly smell.

In the kitchen we stopped suddenly, as though Randi had just realized where we were, and I ended up sitting at a very large table with a red-checked cloth.

Randi took out a salad left over from the previous day. The greens had turned brown at the edges and had yellowish spots and creases, and the tomatoes were exceptionally pale.

She opened a can of asparagus and a can of shrimp, drained the liquid, and added them to the salad.

Then she stood there tossing it as though she were about to fall asleep.

I searched for something to talk about.

Goethe rattled his metal bowl, and a chunk of rye bread rolled out and landed next to my shoe.

Randi chopped an onion, more tomatoes, and a couple of hard-boiled eggs, whose whites were blue or violet or almost black. She threw everything into the salad bowl.

—There, she said.

The original salad was now nearly hidden. She gave it a little toss, then spread out her arms and laughed.

The whole situation felt artificial, when the last thing in the world we wanted was to be strangers to each other.

Now she took out a bigger bowl made of ceramic and glazed in two shades of brown that flowed into each other in a speckled pattern. She poured in plenty of oil, shook in a good amount of wine vinegar, sprinkled in some salt and pepper, and crushed a couple of garlic cloves.

Then she took the bowl in her arms, stirring and continuing the motion, as if dancing, across the wide floor.

—I am so glad you came, she said. So happy, she said, setting down the bowl and kissing me on the forehead.

She snipped a head of lettuce into strips, letting them fall into the dressing.

—It's too bad I didn't throw away the old salad, she said.

—It doesn't matter, I said. You almost can't see the brown spots now.

—Actually, it should marinate a while, Randi said, but we don't have time today.

I must have looked confused because she quickly added:

—I mean since you have to leave so soon. She laughed. To meet Xenia.

—I wish I knew Xenia, I said.

—You can take along her letter, said Randi, heaping salad onto my plate.

She immediately went off to get it as I sat there chew-

ing on a piece of hard bread. It took a long time. So the idea
was that I should take off as soon as we had eaten.

And that's what happened, and when I was out sitting
in the car, Randi said,

—I hope I'll see you again soon.

Goethe barked, and I started the car and called out,

—I'll do what I can.

I drove slowly through the increasingly populated areas
near Uetliberg, where the rain had stopped and the trees
shone in the headlights, making my way onto broader and
longer roads, where the rain had stopped and the asphalt
shone in the headlights, and finally I let myself be pulled
with the current into the city, where the rain . . . where the
city lights were on.

I had almost reached downtown when I realized I was
in the wrong lane, and this was the reason I ended up driving south rather than north. I followed a sign that said
Thalwil-Zug-Lucerne, and drove around the right side of
Lake Zurich.

The road was straight and sang in the mild evening air.
Houses glided by, but mostly flat wide fields glided by,
transforming themselves far out in the semidarkness into
mountains where the rain had presumably also stopped and
the invisible shone in the headlights. I rolled the window
down and sang in the mild evening air.

In Lucerne I particularly remember the river
··············· that sang in the mild evening air.

I was going to stay in Lucerne, but I didn't feel like sleeping yet, so I drove on through a landscape that slowly rose
and fell in the dark, down toward the lights of Brienz, where
the rain had long since stopped and where, from my hotel
room, I could see the lights around Lake Brienz, and remem-

bered the lights around Lake Vierwaldstadt and the lights around another lake whose name I couldn't remember but which sang in the mild evening air. There I lay by the open windows and slept and dreamed.

The next morning I discovered I had come too far west of Passo S. Gottardo 2109. So I drove due east, up over Sustenpass 2224, but when I finally approached the Gotthard area, I was confused by the views and ravines, the bridges and tunnels, glaciers and streams, the commemorative markers for generals apparently of Russian descent, by the cows on the roads, by the flowers called alpine flora among the stones, and in Andermatt, by the police officers, to such a degree that I drove across Oberalppass 2044 instead of across Passo S. Gottardo 2109, and had to continue down through Tschamut and Sedrun with the headwaters of the Rhine far below me, until I reached a slightly larger town of Disentis / Mustér, 1133, where I stopped to ask directions and was told I had to turn due south and drive up over Passo del Lucomagno 1917, which I then did, so at last at Biasca 293 I found the road that would've taken me much more quickly over Passo S. Gottardo 2109, Biasca 293, where the lush Tessin valley with its river and vineyards began to stretch down toward Bellinzona 241, with a scent of Italy beginning, and approaching via Lugano 334, and fully present in the hot, crisp, spicy landscape around the border at Chiasso and Como 201. And now, as you can see, I'm in Rome.

And my dear Katarina, I know you won't be sad or angry when I send you this letter about how I ended up with Xenia's letter, which I am also sending you. You know me!

And you know Xenia.

You once gave her a bouquet of multicolored tulips.

As for me, I've carefully read Xenia's letter here at the Hotel Rome (Via Napoli 3, tel. 484.409–471.565) many times and have arrived at the completely personal conviction that it's a little too well written to have very much to do with the truth.

Probably, if the truth were to come out, Xenia's letter should be called Randi's letter; she's always been quite a liar; I mean Randi, meaning Xenia.

But if the truth is finally to come out, there's one thing that can't have two meanings: Yesterday I was with Azorno here in Rome. It was the first Sunday in May, and the noon hour was unbelievably hot.

*

It was the first Sunday in May and the air was unusually cool. I had just said good-bye to Azorno and wasn't sure which direction to walk now that I was alone after three uninterrupted days with Azorno, who always decides which direction to take; I was especially alone in deciding, determining, ensuring how Sunday would go and in which direction I myself would go since I had said good-bye to Azorno at Track 2 and now stood outside Copenhagen's Central Station looking at the posters in the travel agency windows, at the blue of the sea and sky, particularly the sea that was really a lake lined with houses, all the white houses in all the overwhelming green of the wide, lush lawns that brought out the gleaming letters in Tessin, Lugano, Bellinzona, flowers, flowers, flowers.

The air was unusually cool, time stood unusually still, and I was hungry and went down to the hotdog cart by the main entrance to Tivoli. Two, grilled. Inside Tivoli, people were beginning to stroll down toward the lake and around it. Here and there they stopped, probably to comment on the gardener's vision. Or they loudly expressed their wonder or disappointment about the soundless fountain. I couldn't see that either. The ticket collectors behind the turnstiles behind the woman with the hotdog-colored hair who sold regular and grilled to a long line of customers lining up with other lines of customers in front of the turnstiles in front of the ticket collectors in front of Tivoli with the soundless fountain, which I couldn't see and about which I therefore will not comment.

However, I will gladly comment on the previous sentence: it is not a sentence.

The woman with the hotdog-colored hair said that personally she never eats hotdogs.

On my way back, I bought a bouquet of multicolored tulips that has been in my dining room ever since, reaching out and stretching in all directions. I actually thought that they would stay completely straight since of course I never let a single ray of light disturb me in this room, here where I sit meditating several times a day while eating.

I started on this letter as soon as I had put the tulips in water.

First, I cleaned up after Azorno, his cigarettes and bathrobe, his newspaper, a book. Then I put the tulips in water.

And then I started right away on this letter. Although at first I began meditating in order to find a suitable beginning for it. That is, I began meditating without eating at the same time.

When I realized after a while that I was meditating

without eating at the same time, it occurred to me how improper this was or, at least, unusual for me, and therefore possibly risky, so I went right out and made a cup of coffee and prepared two pieces of white bread with raspberry jam and brought them in here to the dining room on the little white tray I always use when I'm alone, and started right away on this letter.

By this time, the tulips had been in water for a while and a few had already bent and stretched in all directions although I have never let any rays of light disturb me in this room where I sit and eat several times a day while I meditate.

After I had eaten the two pieces of white bread with raspberry jam, I started right away on this letter.

Now it's been several days since I started this letter and I should have told you right away that it was this bouquet of multicolored tulips in particular that got me to start right away on it.

After I had bought them on my way back.

After I had put them in water.

It's now several days later, and as I've been writing and eating while meditating at the same time, the tulips have reached and stretched out in all directions and I have searched my memory to recall whether I have ever given you a bouquet of multicolored tulips.

But, of course, I have never even given you a bouquet of plain tulips.

Of course, I have never given you a bouquet of any kind.

And, my dearest Xenia, you can be completely sure that I never will.

Have I ever given you anything at all?

No. I know that you're allergic to gifts. You can't stand

flowers. You wither up yourself, turn pale, sicken, droop, I understand you so well. Believe me, I understand you so well.

Now I have thrown out the tulips and really ought to start the letter over, but I think that would be going too far, and perhaps these prefatory lines have filled a certain function after all.

Do I dare hope that they have made you understand that I have never, at any point, believed you could have written that incidentally very fine account of the young woman with the white hat whom Azorno meets in Tivoli and who shows a somewhat unusual interest in the tulip beds.

It's ludicrous that it could be you. Ludicrous. Only a person unacquainted with either you or your very highly allergic ways could come up with something so ludicrous. Believe me, I know you too well to fall for this sort of thing. Believe me, I know you too well.

And so I see no reason to rescue you.

On the other hand, now that the tulips were thrown out long ago, I would like to meet here at my place to talk over what we can do to rescue Louise.

You don't know her, true, but her account of the car trip through the Alps is in itself enough to tell you that something is wrong. Only a person who knows she's going to write it down would drive that way.

Or, the only person that would write that way is one who is no longer aware of how she is driving.

To put it briefly, I'm afraid that she is wandering about.

I'm afraid that she is no longer aware of what she is writing nor to whom she is writing.

Believe me, I know how dangerous it is to dream of Azorno. Believe me, I know how dangerous it is. I have known Azorno long enough to realize that it's not dreams that come true.

But, of course, I'm writing first and foremost to you, to assure you that I am very willing to keep you informed about these rumors and their possible course.

About their course, naturally, you can only guess. That Louise says that Randi says that you, my dearest Xenia, started them, is something you shouldn't worry about. Not in the least. Louise has, of course, always been quite a liar.

Other factors may have, of course, come into play, and perhaps you, with your intimate knowledge of these types of symptoms, will be in a position to determine whether there is anything at all in Louise's letter to suggest she may be allergic to the sun.

In which case we would probably come closer to the truth if we forgave her everything. One would need only to hint at it, for example, using matter-of-fact phrasing when declaring her missing. I believe it would sound fine and caring in Italian. She has, as mentioned, taken lodgings in Rome where she is feared to be wandering about due to sunstroke.

*

Dear Bet Sampel: Letting you read through these typewritten letters—well, in my opinion, this typewritten letter, I actually have a strong desire to introduce myself, but I quickly sense that at present that would be superfluous and, moreover, I am afraid that it might seem intrusive. So just call me Xenia!

I am very proud to have found your address. How beautiful it must be to live where you live!

I think I voice the opinion of many readers when I say your husband's ability to live so beautifully and to have such a beautiful wife as his secretary is of the utmost importance to literature.

Your beauty is, of course, a central issue in this matter. Thousands of readers long to have their impressions confirmed, for example, when they read the description of the woman Azorno meets on page eight in Sampel's most recent novel, that these very intense impressions correspond to something in reality, that this beauty really exists, that Sampel's beautiful wife is Sampel's beautiful secretary who is Sampel's beautiful mistress (not to mention Azorno's), a mistress who is simply Sampel's dream of a woman, his dream of a woman in the beautiful house with the beautiful view in beautiful Switzerland near the beautiful lake whose beautiful name is kept secret so that Sampel can cultivate his beautiful rose garden in peace.

I hope you understand this correctly, for I myself am a cultivator of beauty, and I greatly enjoy expressing my experience, my understanding of a book, enjoy doing this on an ordinary basis and with ordinary people; but naturally I find it especially appealing to express myself to the author himself, when my words unfold like a rose—or if for various reasons it is impossible for the author himself to be present, then they unfold like a bouquet of multicolored tulips, one might say, to the author's ubiquitous secretary, who is usually able to give more and fuller replies than the author himself, if he had been present, and if there had been anything at all to ask about.

In the present case, these are certainly not questions of a literary nature.

As we must certainly agree, the hard interests of reality

are at stake. Therefore, it is to put truth simply in its place and to arrive where it rightfully belongs that I am writing to you at all, that I ever in the first place undertook the enormous task of unearthing your address, that I, in connection with this, had to tolerate some publisher's shameless advances, purported to be related to the revelation of secret information, and furthermore, that I, after the second and third time, had to use a great deal of so-called precious time to examine and thoroughly consider the enclosed typewritten letter in order to give you the best possible information about your situation, so this, at any rate, can be considered as it ought to be considered.

I would be pleased if the result of my great effort makes you ask yourself the extremely important question: Has he been unfaithful to me or has he not been unfaithful to me?

I myself have put forward many convincing views. I have taken certain things for granted. First of all, in this case, I have assumed an intimate relationship between the author and his main character, an inextricable relationship infiltrating throughout. The author is not one person and the main character another; Sampel and Azorno are, when it comes down to it, only Sampel, even though Azorno is used all the time; thus, please understand, dear Mrs. Bet, that this letter, which, of course, I am unhappy to have in my possession, not only mentions your husband by his own name, Sampel, but also, and as a rule, mentions him by his main character's name, Azorno, and this last part will most likely give food for thought. For example, I noticed that Katarina cleaned up after Azorno, his cigarettes and bathrobe, his newspapers, a book. Then she put the tulips in water.

Second, I assume that Katarina, at least on this one

point, has spoken the truth. Of course, she is quite a liar, but I have reason to believe her in this case.

It turns out that either she has been right on a number of points—she has always had good intuition—or she has been acting intelligently and sensibly in her own interest.

First and foremost, she immediately knew I never could have written that part of the letter that is attributed to me. I have never known Azorno or any other man and it would not be difficult, though maybe a little complicated, to prove this.

In addition, I believe that Katarina has had good reason to refer to Randi and Louise as zealous man-eaters. The fact is, she herself is not interested.

One evening when she was drinking at my place she gradually became excessively melancholy, and said suddenly that she wanted to seduce Sampel; she promised, she swore an oath on it, and she made me act as a witness; she was completely sober and serious when she got up and swore that she would seduce Sampel. The rest of the evening we spoke at ease about other things. And now I am really convinced that she did it.

And, actually, without any interest. Believe me, she is not interested.

Thus, if you will kindly accept the truth and let it take shelter in your beautiful house—and I should add that it would make me very happy if you would relieve me of it—then, in return, I will help you with all the information you might wish to have, for instance, the addresses of the previously mentioned women, especially, of course, Katarina's, provided, of course, that this time you will undertake the enormous task of finding my address, and in connection with this, eventually endure some publisher's shameless advances purported to be related to secret information concerning yours truly, Xenia.

*

Sampel got up and threw on his bathrobe. The silk shone. He said he heard something, asked if I hadn't heard something, said that he could hear something, asked if I couldn't hear something, said that he heard something now, that he heard someone now, someone, someone on the stone staircase, on the terrace, at the door, on the tiled floor, in the drawing room, in room after room, in the dining room, in the living room, in the sitting room, in the garden room, in the salon, in the tea salon, the smoking salon, the literary salon, in the library, and back again, in the salons, in the rooms, on the tiled floor, the tiled floor at the foot of the stairs, and at any moment by the stairs, on the stairs, and here by the door to the bedroom, where we were lying, had lain, where I was lying, while Sampel was lying and then got up and threw on his bathrobe. The silk shone.

He took it off again. He lay down next to me again. He laid his hand on my breast and my nipple stuck out between his index finger and middle finger. He breathed deeply.

That was the first Sunday in May and the air was pleasant. The shutters were open, so the light moved freely in and out through the tall windows, although not completely freely, never completely freely. One of the windows was so green that it was darkened, was covered by leaves, was sealed from the outside by Virginia creeper and ivy with pale climbing feet that you could just make out on the pane like birds stuck to it, barely visible on the pane behind the climbing rose's vigorous flowers and leaves on a tightly coiled wire frame stretching up from a hole in the floor where the roots of the plant were buried. Stretching up and bouncing like toy clowns on springs, and covering the window on the inside almost more completely than it was covered on the outside, so that it was more difficult to make out the glued bird feet from the inside. It's been said that a woman once threw herself out of this window, without completely killing herself, however. After that, Sampel, in all likelihood, planted this climbing rose with his own hands, that vigorous plant that he, in all likelihood, had with his own hand described in one of his books.

The three other windows also had green vegetation. Of course, there were no curtains or any valances at the top, only a little shelf for each window on which were placed nine small flower pots with baby's tears, a plant with stalks so thin, leaves so small, yet altogether the plants were so dense and long that it seemed they could be combed like hair. Three times nine small women's heads with their faces toward the wall and the heavy green hair falling completely freely down into the space before the windows, although never completely freely. He turned my nipple around like he was adjusting a radio dial. I picked a little at the sheet near his head, stroked his hair, and ran the tips of my fingers around and around in the folds of his left ear, while I hummed with my mouth close to his ear. Like a radio station that fades out and disappears. Dies. Is dead. But breathing, deep, deep inside the body.

Sampel got up and threw on his bathrobe. The light filtered through the women's hair. The air was green. I could clearly hear that someone was coming. On the stone staircase. On the terrace. It's her, he whispered. By the door. On the tiled floor. Don't move. For all the world, don't move.

Play dead. Now he was standing at the door to the stairs. She, at the door to the drawing room. She, in room after room. He, already on the stairs. She, in the dining room. He, on the stairs. She, in the living room, the sitting room. He, on the tiled floor at the foot of the stairs. She, in the garden room. He, in room after room. She, in the salon. He, in the dining room. She, in the tea salon. He, in the living room, sitting room. She, in the smoking salon. He, in the garden room. She, in the literary salon. He, in the salon. She, in the library and back again. He, in the tea salon. She, in the literary salon. He, in the smoking salon, she, in the smoking salon, he and she, in the tea salon, in the salon, in the garden room, in the sitting room, the drawing room, talking, in the dining room, in room after room, on the tiled floor, the tiled floor at the foot of the stairs, and at any moment on the staircase and right here outside the door to the bedroom where I lay while Sampel got up and threw on his bathrobe, and now he was standing with her on the tiled floor at the foot of the stairs talking and talking like a radio station that at last fades out and disappears. Dies. Is dead. Breathing, deep, deep inside the body, while I am listening: Maybe I hear him turning her nipple around like he's adjusting a radio dial.

It fell completely silent. I felt like a diver who finds himself at the bottom of the ocean one minute and on solid ground the next, unable to hear whether the others are saying he's alive or dead because he's encapsulated in a silence as vast as if he'd brought the ocean up with him and it surrounded him now like a huge bell that no one could pass through without drowning. The fluttering plant curtains filtered the light that flickered over my eyelids as over a gray sandy bottom. I dozed off in this air that was dense and warm and green, and also poisonous, because she had already discovered me, and then, with the greatest silence, sprayed her poison in through the windows, a green poison that quickly stripped all the leaf-flesh off my human body, exposing my ribs, fluids, and reproductive system, causing me to cave in, collapse, crumble, almost vanish; yes, there was actually only a little dust remaining, and that could be easily brushed off the sheet before lying down, as if there were a little sand between the toes the evening before. I got up. A couple of drops fell from my crotch. They spread out and became a little gray spot on the sheet. A little head with ears.

Why couldn't she hear me? Couldn't Sampel go to bed with all the women who happened to cross his path? Incidentally, why didn't he come back? Maybe I really wasn't all that interested.

I got all the way up and went over to the window. The plants spread out over my shoulders like an extension of my hair. There was nothing to see. I mean, no one to see. No one to hear. The lake was deep and shining, just as the sky was deep and shining. And the mountains on the other side were reflected across the entire lake so that there was no place for the sky to reflect in, at least not from this vantage point; the mountains were deep and shining.

I turned around and saw that they were reflected in the mirror over Bet Sampel's dressing table, so that she, with this deep and shining background, could sit and look into her own deep and shining eyes. I sat down and moved my hands around the many creams and cosmetics. I opened a couple of jars and closed them again. Most of them had screw caps. One bottle had a greasy ribbon around its neck. I fiddled a bit with most of them, put some perfume on the back of one hand and some lotion on the other, used gobs of cream on my breasts and began to paint my mouth, first cyclamen, then beige, then scarlet, and then rubbed it all off. Then I brushed my hair, combed it behind my ears, and saw that I had accidentally made a middle part, a kind of perfect symmetry with the mountains as background. I found a bra in one of her drawers and put it on; it was a size too big. And a pair of light green silk pants with three small lace flowers and a slit on the left side. They were a size too small and looked ridiculous. Then I carefully painted my mouth again so that it looked like a pitted dried apricot, and painted my eyes as well with their nearer and more distant features, so that at last when I looked into them, they seemed quite deep and shining against the background of the mountains that were also deep and shining.

Then when the image was complete I blew life into it with a cigarette holder, and when I was looking around for cigarettes in order to get the entire machinery of the artwork to work, I happened to find Xenia's letter to Bet Sampel. Nothing could've gotten it to work more perfectly. I lit a cigarette and read it. I lit another cigarette and read it again. It could've been Bet Sampel herself indignantly lighting one cigarette after another while reading this letter. Then, suddenly, footsteps on the stairs. Crumple up the letter. Away. The door opens. Sampel steps in. I am nonchalantly smoking the cigarette in the cigarette holder with my gaze turned toward the mountains on the other side.

Sampel laughs. Grabs the cigarette and rubs it into the rug, with his heel he stamps the cigarette holder to pieces, and then he tears the bra and silk pants off me while yelling so that it echoes off the deep shining mountains on the other side of the lake: I'm free. I'm free! Bet Sampel can paddle her own canoe. Along with her deep and shining eyes. And then he licked my eyelashes with his long, rough tongue and spit out the mix of garish colors onto the white silk wallpaper. I'm free, he said. I'm free. And I was terrified that he would lap up my eyes. Darling, darling Randi, I'm free, now we can always be together. Now. Now. Now.

I really wasn't all that interested.

Sampel might have suspected this because he watched me day in and day out and probably no longer had time to write his books.

I even had to write at night while he slept and, naturally, when it was dark, so that words and lines often tangled with each other and became difficult to decipher, but in a way, this happened to correspond with the dark that suddenly no longer only surrounded me at night but also pressed in on me in the daytime, and in this way was able to watch me, thus relieving Sampel, giving him time to write his books, while I sat at the overgrown window thinking about Xenia's letter concerning all of us, and about the small glued-down birds' feet behind the blackened leaves.

I'm afraid of Xenia's letter to Bet Sampel, and don't want it.

I'm afraid of Katarina's letter to Xenia, and don't want it.

I'm afraid of Louise's letter to Katarina, and don't want it.

I'm afraid of my own letter, and don't want it.

Is my memory correct when I think I heard you are wandering around Rome while I'm locked up here?

Is my memory correct when I think you are unusually good at driving on mountain roads?

Is my memory correct when I think I remember you?

Louise, Rome, Via Napoli 3, tel: 484.409–471.565.

Is my memory correct when I think you remember me

and would like to drive back over the border at Como
Chiasso 201 and via Lugano 334, leaving the hot, crisp,
spicy landscape that still has a scent of Italy, arriving at
Bellinzona 241, where the lush Tessin valley, with its river
and vineyards, stretches up toward Biasca 293, where you
can't decide whether to drive up over Passo S. Gottardo
2109 or over Passo del Lucomagno 1917, and where I
believe you are choosing the latter, stopping to ask for
directions at Disentis / Mustér, 1133, and, with the Rhine
far below, you continue up toward Tschamut and Sedrun
and in over Oberalppass 2044 and from here you glide easily through Andermatt and up over Sustenpass 2224, where
the rain has probably stopped so that you can roll down the
window and sing in the mild evening air.

   You don't want to sleep yet, and while you drive slowly
on through the landscape that rises and falls in the dark,
you remember the lights, the lights around Lake Brienz, and
remember the lights around Lake Vierwaldstadt, and the
lights along another lake whose name you can't remember,
but that I hope you'll be able to find while you sing in the
mild evening air so you can find me. And save me. From
this place where I sit looking out over the lake, which is neither very deep nor shining. The same holds true for the sky.
And the mountains. And last but not least, my eyes.

   For now I am Sampel's prisoner, in this place where
darkness spreads with the speed of light.

*

When I first began working on this novel I actually did live
in Rome, Via Napoli 3.

   Louise _____, at present, Rome, Via Napoli 3, I wrote
at the top of each and every sheet of paper, including, as a
rule, my telephone number: 484.409–471.565.

It was a habit I had from when I wrote letters as often and painstakingly as you wash your hands. Several times a day.

Of course, the number of letters I received was in no way as great as the number I sent.

For every hundred letters I sent off I could expect to receive ten.

But the hundred letters sent were all very personal, whereas only four of the ten letters I received had that same personal character.

These four . . .

Yes, what riches.

But these four always included one from some person I could never bring myself to write back to, and two were from relatives or other acquaintances, and only one, one single letter, was actually a reply to one of the hundred I had written.

However it was almost always a reply to one I had written a long time ago, three or four hundred letters back and, therefore, one I could no longer remember.

And that one letter . . .

Yes, what riches.

It was immediately clear that this single letter that should be a reply to more than one hundred letters, didn't include a single answer, but, on the contrary, included only detailed explanations about why this person couldn't give me an answer, unfortunately couldn't give me an answer, was not in a position to give me an answer at the moment.

This was the type of answer that would immediately get me to come up with thousands of questions and to write letters without interruption.

But not when I lived in Rome, Via Napoli 3.

No one knew that address. No one should know it. No one should know where I was. No one knew.

And all the many sheets of paper that I inscribed at the top with my name and that address were never used for writing letters but to write this novel, which, at least to begin with, definitely had the form of a series of letters, though I never intended that they be put in envelopes and mailed like letters: you might look at the whole thing as a result of the habit I had when I wrote letters as often and painstakingly as you wash your hands. Several times a day.

Several times a day, the first thing in the morning, I wrote on one sheet after the other: Louise _____, at present, Rome, Via Napoli 3.

It was a street that left me in peace. I could eat and sleep in peace. I could distract myself watching my neighbors in peace. And I could work on this novel. In peace. Everything was in the most perfect order. I escaped here precisely to be left in peace.

In the beginning it was actually not my intention to use this peace merely for something as simple as eating and sleeping, watching neighbors, and writing novels.

It had been my sole intention, in fact, the whole way down here I was firmly resolved, that the peace should be used only for working out an accurate explanation of the actions that led to this escape to peace.

But it quickly became clear that there could be no explanation for my actions, only an explanation of my lack of actions. To be more precise, the goal would be to find an explanation for actions I had announced a long time ago, but left undone for an even longer time, for events that never occurred in the order I had planned, or in any other order for that matter, for events that simply failed to occur

and that were omitted from the plan I had outlined.
Outlined for others. The others to whom I would therefore
give an explanation. Which is why I escaped down here to
be in peace.

I drank my coffee in a downstairs bar with the others
from the street. I didn't look at them because they weren't
to think that I wanted to look at them. Most of the time
there was an old floor rag that I could look at. It would
twitch on the tiled floor, licking the yellow and blue until
the floor became shiny and appetizing.

I usually went to get another cup of coffee, with down-
cast eyes so they could see that I didn't see them.

When the floor rag wasn't there I picked at an old sandstone sculpture, a little greenish manikin with oversized ears
and waves down the chest as on a washboard to signify
frizzy hair. It sat on a shelf in a niche that was painted blue.
I had picked a little hole in his right thigh without anyone
seeing me. And all the while I thought about what I should
write on this or that sheet of paper, which in the morning I
had inscribed with my name: Louise _____, at present,
Rome, Via Napoli 3.

Xenia, Randi, Katarina, and Bet Sampel, and, for that
matter, both Sampel and Azorno, all had the right to an
explanation.

Of course, an explanation was nothing they would
demand. They've always been far too sensitive to ask for
anything. As a whole, they were not used to making
demands, and if, despite all possible precautions, they came
close to anything that seemed to be a demand, they quickly
turned it against themselves. Never on others. They dug
inward. With their great sensitivity they turned loose on
their own soft flesh and dug out portions of themselves to

make room for more. They made room for everything I told them, opening up for every little story, sucking in every word, every detail, continuously making room for what was to come. For the next lie.

And I let them sacrifice themselves. Satiated them.

Then I escaped here to write in peace. Every morning I wrote my name at the top of the paper: Louise _____, at present, Rome, Via Napoli 3.

Then I drank coffee while I looked at the floor rag and the little sandstone sculpture.

Then I climbed up from the bar, bought grapes from the usual stand, and took them up to my room.

Then I closed the window and looked at the man in the room across the way.

When he was finished washing himself and dressing behind the door of the wardrobe so that I wouldn't see him, and had left the room, and when I had seen him leave the building, I sat down at the desk with the day's sheets of paper to begin my explanation.

First I would work out a general explanation.

Then I would explain everything to Xenia.

Then I would explain everything to Randi, in general terms.

Then I would explain everything in general to Katarina, and, in particular, my escape.

Then I would explain everything in general to Bet Sampel, and, in particular, my escape to Rome, Via Napoli 3.

Would then explain to Sampel.

Would then explain Sampel.

Explain Azorno

Explain

Plain

In

In the late afternoon, at five o'clock, I went out again.

If I hadn't already gone out at twelve o'clock or three o'clock. Stopped at random shops. Thought about buying a hat. A white hat. Walked on. Walked back. Walked over to the opposite sidewalk and stood and waited under an awning. Walked away nonetheless. Went on my way. By chance came back to the window with the white hat. Thought about buying it. Walked on. Walked back. Walked on. Walked back. Walked on. Walked or practically ran back to my room and slept.

Or I didn't go out at five o'clock, but at nine o'clock in the evening. Without a hat or gloves. With a dark dress against my dark skin against the dark evening. Only my teeth were shining when I opened my mouth, and the whites of my eyes, if I didn't lower them, and very faintly the nails of my ungloved dark hands.

With tight lips, half-closed eyes, and my nails sunk into my palms I sat hiding at the edge of a large circular fountain that, splashing, caught all of the jets of water used for rinsing off the women and swans placed in their calculated positions in the middle of the Piazza della Repubblica after being carved in stone. I hid in the dense row of people occupying the edge of the fountain. This dense human row was part of the dense human mass occupying the entire square that was in motion like a necklace on the earth's bosom, being hit by beams of light, rays, in flashes, glinting like lightning—a few women in white hats, men in white shirts against dark skin.

How much had I told them? I dragged my fingers through the lukewarm water and thought about how much I'd told each person, how much I'd told some and not the others, how much I'd told one and not the others, and how much each one then told the others and not me, how much they all told one another and not me.

How in the world to take control over the progression of a story that from the beginning has simply contained a concealed desire to communicate something that would catch their attention, but then turned out to be to their liking, to such an extent that they swallowed it raw and later had to throw up the indigestible remains and, in the company of friends and acquaintances, regard them as the consequences of an incomprehensible but harmless disease. In this way I quickly lost touch with my story, and what began on my part as a downright lie could easily slide toward something seriously close to the truth.

The man who dressed behind the door of the wardrobe passed by. I buried my nails in my hand and decided to slip unseen out of the dense row of people at the edge of the fountain and sneak back to my room where I would not put on the light or wash myself, but simply hurry into bed.

Or I didn't go out at nine o'clock in the evening, or at five or three o'clock in the afternoon. I went out only in the morning. Without a hat or gloves. Didn't see my neighbor get up and dress. Didn't see him in the evening in a white shirt between the cars in the Piazza della Repubblica. Still did not turn on the light when I finally got back to my room and didn't wash myself either, but went to bed with the scent of the mass of people still clinging to my skin.

This mass of people . . .

Yes.

Over on the table lay the white sheet of paper with its Louise _____, at present, Rome, Via Napoli 3.

The whole thing probably began when I told Randi that

I was in love with Azorno. About the same time I told Randi that Azorno was in love with me.

I told Bet Sampel that Azorno made a pass at me and tried to be alone with me every chance he got.

And I told Sampel repeatedly that I never went to bed with anyone other than Azorno.

I told Xenia that Azorno had straight out raped me.

I turned and kicked the bedspread off. I can't be without him, I murmured. And I tried to kick the heat off but it was too heavy.

I was pregnant. Or I wished that I was pregnant. Or I had wished that I was pregnant. Or I had said that I was. Maybe I had thought that I could be just by saying it. Saying it to the others. To all of them. Until they believed it. Until I myself believed it.

Or I would first go out at night, after I had worked all day on the novel. I got out of bed and dressed without turning on the light. Over on the table lay the sheets of paper ready for the next morning: Louise _____, at present, Rome, Via Napoli 3, tel. 484.409–471.565.

This mass of people . . .

A few of whom were still strolling in the streets.

What would they have said when they saw that I wasn't getting bigger?

What did Azorno say when he heard about it? Was he so flattered that he didn't reveal that he'd never been to bed with me? Did he have reasons that I'm unaware of for not revealing that he hadn't gotten me pregnant?

In any case, it's more than likely that they continued my story for me while I was away.

They expanded and improved it. Made it more realistic. Xenia, Randi, Katarina, and Bet knit small clothes for

Azorno's child. And Azorno had already bought a baby carriage although he knew very well that I wasn't pregnant, but still hoped that I was by someone else, and especially hoped I preferred it had been by him, so I would never reveal I wasn't by anyone.

Rather than intervening at this point, stopping the whole story, telling them the situation, sending my letters as I used to and openly writing: All of it is lies. I'm not pregnant. I'm not in love. I don't know him, etc.—rather than preventing the whole story from living its own life, I simply began a new story. A different story.

Every morning I wrote at the top of the sheet of paper: Louise _____, at present, Rome, Via Napoli 3, and went out. After I had coffee in the downstairs bar and watched the man across the way get dressed behind the wardrobe and go out, I sat down to work on this novel that I had started, and then went out again at five or three o'clock in the afternoon, nine o'clock in the evening, or late, late in the evening, after I had slept, without a hat or gloves, in the hot streets where only a few were left from the mass of people.

Someday when Xenia, Randi, Katarina, Bet Sampel, Sampel, and Azorno are allowed to read this novel they'll be so shocked to see themselves as characters in it that they'll completely forget to ask about Azorno's child. The small articles of clothing will disappear by themselves, and the baby carriage will just sit there not belonging to anyone.

That baby carriage . . .

Yes.

Or I would go out at twelve o'clock, noon. When he had finished washing and dressing himself behind the door of the wardrobe so that I wouldn't see him, and had left the room, and when I had seen him leave the building, I sat down at the desk with the day's sheets of paper and began to work on this novel. Sat looking at my name: Louise _____, at present, Rome, Via Napoli 3.

Or I would get up and follow him through the hot streets in the evening, hiding myself in the middle of the Piazza della Repubblica where from my place at the edge of the fountain I saw him pass by in a white shirt against his dark skin against the dark evening.

Or I would first go out late at night, after I had slept, with the scent of the warm mass of people lingering on my skin. After I had worked on this novel all day.

Or I would only go out in the morning and wouldn't return the whole day. After I slept with the man in the room across the way and watched him get up and wash himself and get dressed, not as he usually did behind the door of the wardrobe, but right in front of the bed so I could see him, and after he had left the room. And the building. I went out and drank coffee while looking at the floor rag and that little sandstone sculpture.

Then I climbed up from the bar, bought grapes at the usual stand, and took them up to my room.

Or, as already mentioned, I would go out only in the morning and wouldn't come back.

*

Of course, I didn't live in Rome, Via Napoli 3, when I began working on this novel.

I lived on Helgolands Street. But every time I wrote Katarina—Helgolands Street, Copenhagen, at the top of the white sheet of paper, it looked so imposing that I couldn't find a single word for my novel.

Therefore I wrote Louise _____, at present, Rome, Via Napoli 3 instead. And this helped. It pleased me to use Louise as a narrator. She's always been a good storyteller and that's more than I can say about myself.

I can sit alone for several days without saying a word.

Without saying a single one of all the words that exist.

But of course I can be forced to make a comment.

In the evening as I eat and meditate while being watched by the cat, suddenly I can become afraid that he might jump on me and, in anger over my muteness, start scratching at my mouth in order to rip out a couple of words; if it happens that I can't overcome my fear in any other way, I make a couple of soothing sounds between mouthfuls and he immediately starts to purr, making me feel comfortable again so that I can be alone for several more days without saying a word.

After I had sat alone in this way a whole week and still had no desire to see the people I knew, it suddenly occurred to me that I could write about the people I knew. I could make them dance around with one another here on the dining-room table. Make them stretch out in all directions like the multicolored tulips that haven't had any light. Make them wither and die. But above all, I could make them be present without the trouble of having to feed or serve them in any way and, at the same time, their illusory presence would entertain the cat, thus preventing his attack on my muteness.

After it occurred to me that I could write this novel, I made a couple of soothing sounds to the cat and went out at twelve o'clock. I stopped outside Copenhagen's Central Station to look at the posters in the travel agency windows, the blue of sea and sky, particularly the sea that was really a lake lined with houses, all the white houses in all the overwhelming green of the wide, lush lawns that brought out the gleaming letters in Tessin, Lugano, Bellinzona. On the way home I bought a bouquet of multicolored tulips and put them in water, all the while thinking how lovely it would be to be in Tessin, Lugano, Bellinzona writing this novel—flowers, flowers, flowers.

After I had sat alone for another week and still had no desire to see anyone I knew, I went out at three o'clock to buy paper the right size and quantity on which to write this novel. About the people I knew. On the way home I bought a bouquet of multicolored tulips to replace the bouquet of multicolored tulips that had withered. And I put them in water.

After I had sat alone for three weeks and had figured out that those people I knew were Randi, Xenia, Louise, Bet Sampel, Sampel, and Azorno, I wrote their names down on a piece of paper so as not to forget that I wanted to write this novel about them. After I had sat alone in this way for three weeks and had written down all of their names and had my fight with the cat, I went out at five o'clock.

It was raining. I bought a red umbrella and went into Tivoli where I sat at a table and ordered two Camparis. I pulled the table toward me so that my feet and legs all the way up to my thighs and crotch were hidden under the round tabletop, and I sat with a straight back and open umbrella and paid the waiter as soon as he brought the two Camparis under my red sky. The rain buzzed around me. Almost considerately. I drank one of the Camparis, holding the little lemon slice up against the gray sky. Ate it. Drank the second Campari, went home, and placed the umbrella in the corner of the dark dining room.

After I had sat alone in the dining room and had eaten

and meditated for four weeks, fighting on and off with the cat, I figured out that Louise was the person best suited for the role of the narrator, the first-person narrator, in this novel I was going to write about the people I knew, and when the paper I'd ordered in the size and quantity I wanted arrived at last, I wrote her name at the top of one sheet after another and went out at nine o'clock in the evening just to return immediately.

The cat was sleeping. He was lying in the middle of the bed, my bed, in the middle of the bedroom, my bedroom, past the dining room where I stood completely still. I tiptoed over and closed the door and sat down very quietly at the table to write. Everything was now in the most perfect order. It was a very good dining room on a very good street. Helgolands Street.

It was a street that left me in peace. I could eat and sleep in peace. I could distract myself watching my neighbors in peace, but of course only from the living room where I never went because I wanted to be in peace. And I could work on this novel. In peace. I had locked the door to the bedroom and sat picking at the wilted tulip petals. They lay shining under the light like that on dark residential streets one evening in June when driving slowly by. If I had saved all the petals from the many bouquets, tulip petal by tulip petal, in a colorful heap, and if they had kept their freshness, and if I had bought even more, if I had shook them a little so that the petals fell off, if I had bought them all at one time, and if I had shook them so that the petals all fell off . . .

What riches . . .

The cat was awake and scratching at the door. I sat as still as a mouse. Then he leaped up and dragged his front paws all the way down. I went over to the door and tentatively let a couple of soothing sounds slip in through the crack. He then began to leap around the room, scratching here and there in a mad frenzy.

I could hardly breathe and didn't know what to do.

In order to lessen my anxiety I went into the kitchen and made a cup of coffee and two pieces of white bread with raspberry jam and brought them into the living room on a little white tray that I always use when I'm alone. I'm very fond of being alone. I wish to be alone. I eat my two pieces of white bread with raspberry jam. I am not in love anymore. I sit very still and wish for nothing more. Hope for nothing more. Eat. Eat my two pieces of white bread. Am not in love anymore. With raspberry jam.

My heart was beating hard as I sat at the bottom of the dark staircase waiting for him to pass by. He could've stumbled over me, given me a kick, or, if I hung onto his pant leg, stomped on my hands until they bled. At last one evening after I had faithfully sat there for several weeks he sent for the police and they came and got me and put me away and locked the door until I learned little by little to be alone.

The night passed. It was quiet. Gradually it became absolutely quiet. It was completely soundless. I felt like a diver who finds himself at the bottom of the ocean one minute and on solid ground the next, unable to hear whether the others are saying he's alive or dead because he's encapsulated in a silence as vast as if he'd brought the ocean up with him and it surrounded him now like a huge bell that no one could pass through without drowning. In that silence. Yes. I dozed. Dozing as still as a mouse. After that, over the course of the night, several of my bottles and jars of creams and cosmetics fell off the dressing table. Then a lamp, a vase, a glass bottle. I dozed. Quietly. The cat was possibly ready to pounce. And was encapsulated in the same way by silence. If I so much as breathed heavily, if I licked my lips to moisten them, if I simply dozed off with an open mouth, if I dreamed, dreamed that I got up and opened that red umbrella and floated over the multicolored tulips that stretched and bent in all directions, then these sounds would be followed by others, like, for example, the sound from the window shattering in the bedroom. The tinkling of breaking glass. Somewhere a door slamming. The umbrella sliding slowly down from its leaning position in a corner of the dining room. I got up to make coffee. Spread two pieces of white bread with raspberry jam for the cat. And brought them into the dining room on a little white tray, which I always use when I'm alone.

After I had sat alone in the dining room in this way for four weeks, I armed myself with two pieces of white bread with raspberry jam, unlocked the door to the bedroom, and, uttering an adequate number of soothing sounds, went in to the cat, which, as it turned out, had been gone for a long time. A pane of glass was shattered where he had jumped out. The curtains were torn. It was already light. I opened the window and called out. In the same moment the cat leaped from the enclosed courtyard and in a long curve flew right in through the broken pane over my head and dropped down around me like the flowers on that dark residential street one evening in June when driving slowly by. I took a step back speechless with terror, fell over a lamp, and tumbled onto the bed. He quietly licked my eyelids with his large, rough tongue, and I was afraid that he would lap up my eyes. I made a couple of soothing sounds, and he gradually began to purr so that I could feel safe again and regain the stamina to sit alone for several days without saying a word.

After I had sat alone for five weeks, I went out at precisely twelve o'clock. It was raining. I bought a green umbrella and went into Tivoli and sat at a table and ordered two Dubonnets. I pulled the table toward me and sat with a straight back and open umbrella and paid the waiter as soon as he brought the two Dubonnets under my green sky. The rain buzzed around me. Almost considerately. I drank my two Dubonnets, went home, and placed the umbrella in water on the dining-room table where I sat several times a day to eat and meditate and begin writing this novel.

After I had figured out that the people I knew were Randi, Xenia, Louise, Bet Sampel, Sampel, and Azorno, after I furthermore had figured out that Louise was the person best suited for the role of narrator, the first-person narrator, after I had placed that green umbrella in water, after I had placed the red umbrella in water in the same way, after I had finally cleaned up after the cat and picked up the cigarettes, bathrobe, newspapers, a book, and after I had at last eaten the two pieces of white bread with raspberry jam, I went out at exactly three o'clock.

When I got back, Louise was there. She had let herself in and was sitting at the dining-room table with the cat on her lap. She didn't really have him on her lap, rather he lay across her thighs, and the four cat paws and tail clutched and wrapped around her stomach, which was rather large. She had closed the umbrella and put it in the corner of the dining room, and in the middle of the table she had placed a bouquet of multicolored tulips that were already bending and stretching in all directions.

I said I was happy to receive the tulips.

She said that she was happy about her condition.

I then asked her if she wanted a cup of coffee, and who the father of the child was.

She said that she had just gotten back from Rome and there were so many it could be. I said that was exciting, and, she said, yes, she would like to have two pieces of white bread with raspberry jam. We ate and chatted about Rome, about Randi and Xenia, Bet Sampel and Sampel, about Azorno, about mutual acquaintances, the people I knew, the novel I ought to begin, and the multicolored tulips that bent and stretched in all directions while we ate and chatted.

After we had eaten two pieces of white bread with raspberry jam, we went out at five o'clock. Exactly five o'clock. It was still raining. We bought a blue umbrella and went into Tivoli where we sat at a table and ordered two martinis. I pulled the table toward me all the way and it still touched her stomach, and so we sat with straight backs and an open umbrella and paid the waiter as soon as he brought the two martinis under our blue sky. The rain buzzed around us. Almost considerately. We drank our martinis and left. I went home and put the umbrella in the corner with the other two. Then I made an appointment with a glazier to put new panes in the window in the bedroom, and a stonemason to lay blue and yellow tiles in the enclosed courtyard, and to put in a fountain that would splash with a tone other than rain. Then I sat at the table in the dining room and began writing this novel.

*

The fountain splashed. Babbled. The jet of water in the middle of the circular fountain rose and fell in one motion, rose up as through a plant stem that has long been thirsty, then immediately turned into an open flower and fell again, petal after petal, sprinkling down and shattering.

Or it rose like a resistant glass tube sent vertically into the air from the reclining glassblower's mouth, at the peak of his strength, foaming like a collar that glides out to form a full skirt, without ever being flung like arms in a swift gesture, without ever dancing.

Or rose. And fell. Like green plants' green hair. Their long hair. Like long hair in a completely free fall down through space. Although, never completely freely. Always a little sticky. Like hair that clings to the skin, that clings to the body, that clings to blood. That rises. Rose. And falls. Fell.

Or splashed. Babbled. Settling on its source and mumbling over and over the first words it has learned.

Or sang in the mild evening air.

In the enclosed courtyard.

Where I sat on the low stone bench in the colonnade and dozed. Listened. Wished that I could in the same way babble and mumble in a language I didn't know or understand, and was not going to use to pin down and determine my actions. My next actions. Wished not to act. Wished to doze in the language, letting it spout like a fountain where opposing sources stream from all sides, rising and spouting forth. Wished that the language would leave me in peace, keeping three steps behind, and there, right in the middle, present its tricks, juggling, fire breathing, dancing, making music, singing, and balancing on multicolored balls and, above all, self-assuredly raising itself as swaying acrobatic pyramids.

And these tricks should be so strenuous that every word has to be in its place, and stretched to its outermost limit. A language that functions perfectly without my help, or intervention. I wished for this. To buy time. To prevent a rash decision. Dozing.

I jumped up when the phone rang. Ready to run and get it. Ran for it. But didn't dare pick it up. Let it ring seven times while I slowly walked back and sat down on the stone bench. The fountain splashed. Overwhelmingly. Insisting loudly. Buzzing in my ears. Now I was sorry about my hesitation. A failure I regret. Sitting on the stone bench, actually needing to confide in someone.

I saw that a little water mixed with dirt had seeped in under the door that connects the enclosed courtyard with the garden. It was as though a bleeding man were lying on the path out there, most likely across the path with his head under the wide rhubarb leaves.

Splashed. Buzzing in my ears.

I went and shut off the tap. The jets of water sank down. The surface of the water became calm and that dark metallic mouth became visible in the basin. In that slimy basin. Like a gun. Sent vertically into the air from the reclining glass-blower's mouth. The assassin's hand.

I could hear the rain out in the garden. I lit a cigarette and leaned against the wall next to the sandstone sculpture. The little manikin swayed a bit. I took it by the arm and blew smoke over its lifeless eyes. A snail that had been sitting in the frizzy beard rolled down onto the tiles and landed wrong side up. The puddle by the door had grown larger and was now the same dark color as the metallic nozzle in the middle of the basin.

I thought I might be freezing.

When the phone rang again, I threw the sculpture down and leaped so as not to trip over it, took the wide stone stairs two at a time with the help of a kind of climbing grip carved into the banister.

Yes, I said, out of breath. Yes. Yes. The operator gave me different bits of information. I was about to say yes, and stubbed out my cigarette on the wall. It left a black mark on the whitewash.

Yes, this is Randi, I said, and repeated it until I was sure I knew to whom I was speaking. Later I realized how unwise it was to reveal my name without knowing who it was, maybe a dangerous enemy. But I said yes, and said it again immediately, yes, yes this is Randi, yes.

The black cigarette mark on the whitewash was right by an old portrait, or more precisely, right by the nose of an unkown man in profile who was drawn on the dull paper- with such a thin and black line, then framed and hung on the wall here in the gallery. At one time. I called him the composer. His kind expression was directly aimed at the mark. He's always had his place here over the dark oak chest, the one with a squared recess carved into the curved lid as if to accomodate the phone. Some time ago. Later, the paper became dull, the oak dark, and the telephone was put in, although there was never much light in the gallery. There isn't now either. Here you could comfortably forget to whom you were talking and focus only on the composer, his eyes, his mouth. Hear his music.

Yes, I'm comfortable, I said, and sat up on the chest with my feet pressed against the row of rosettes that lined the lid.

And then Katarina told me all about Louise.

It grew into a very long, and actually, a very sad story,

which I'm completely incapable of retelling, mainly because I object to Katarina's way of presenting it. She didn't speak about Louise, but about Louise's character.

The sunset had ended somewhere far beyond the rain and mountains. By the way, I don't think Katarina was even trying to get close to the truth, if, once again, just for a moment, I consider the truth to be the actual circumstances.

At the end of the story was the frightening revelation that the story itself was precisely the reason for my being asked to drive as quickly as possible up through Germany, because Katarina, on account of this whole story, etc., needed me, etc., etc. It was said in three minutes. Do you want to know more? she asked.

—Yes, I said. What do you mean? I asked.

—Well, said Katarina, I wanted to ask you to rescue Louise.

—What do you mean? I said, sounding more foolish than before.

—Well, said Katarina, you have to help her understand that she's caught in a daydream.

—How could that be? I said helplessly.

—Well, said Katarina, you must explain everything to her, tell her that I was with Sampel the other day, and that he told me I'm the woman whom the main character in his novel meets on page eight.

What do you mean? I almost said, but stopped myself.

—And do you know who the main character is, the man? continued Katarina. It's Azorno.

—But what, I asked, do you want me to do?

—Well, there's a lot to do, said Katarina. They've locked her up.

—How? I said.

—She's been hospitalized.

—Yes.

—She's being held involuntarily.

—Yes. I mean, yes.

—And she keeps mentioning you again and again.

—Does she? Why?

—Randi, she says, I'll never forget Randi, even though they're keeping her locked up.

—Keeping me locked up? I said.

Katarina said that Louise, from her confinement, tried to rescue me time after time from my confinement.

I said that I would try to reciprocate and, as quickly as possible, drive up through Germany.

Outside, the rain beat with another tone. I packed. Most of my belongings were already in the suitcase from last time. At the bottom were the finished sections of the novel with related used and unused notes. On top of that was a multicolored heap of extra bras, girdles, panties, stockings, sandals, scarves, gloves, creams, cosmetics, and a white hat, all rolled up in a glossy transparent plastic tube with a handle made of twisted gold thread. In a little mesh bag, two blouses and one dress were crumpled together and yet, even in this condition, they were ready to use because they were made of artificial fabric. I filled the holes and spaces in between with writing pads of different sizes, until I more or less had a flat surface about five centimeters under the lid of the suitcase. On this flat part I put the unfinished sections of the novel with its related used and unused notes.

Then I started the car and drove slowly through the increasingly populated areas of Uetliberg, where the rain had stopped and the trees shone in the headlights, making my way onto broader and longer roads, where the rain had stopped and the asphalt shone in the headlights, and finally I let myself be pulled with the current into the city, where the rain . . . where the city lights were on.

The city glided by and settled behind my car that glided on and adjusted itself to the road that was now completely straight and sang in the mild evening air. Houses glided by, but mostly flat wide fields glided by, transforming themselves far out in the semidarkness into mountains where the rain had presumably also stopped and the invisible shone in the headlights. I rolled down the window and sang in the mild evening air.

It was a question of a release. Having to solve a problem, especially a problem related to a confinement, was an immediate relief to me. I breathed easier being forced to breathe in order to move, in order to solve a problem, especially a problem related to the confinement of another person, in this case, one of my friends, a woman no less, and, in this case, the woman I, on top of everything, had chosen to be the first-person narrator of my novel, Louise, Via Napoli 3, but who was unfortunately confined and therefore replaced by Katarina, Katarina, at Helgolands Street, who, in the meantime, had committed herself so fervently to Louise's release, that she, on top of everything, had asked me to drive as fast as possible up through Germany to help, which subsequently I did, am doing, even though at the same time, I had to become my own narrator in my own novel because of Louise's and Katarina's indisposition.

It was a question of gentleness. Solving something for others that can't be solved for yourself demands, first and foremost, that you refrain from using any sharp objects, which no one wants to be cut with anyway. The problem

therefore can be solved in two ways: with poison or freedom. Both equally gently. Every confinement can terminate
from within: e.g., by giving the tree poison and quickly paralyzing the tissues in their multiple functions. When everything stands still in this way, a mute block, all movement
begins to go downward: flowers disintegrate, leaves curl up,
rustle, are carried away, twigs on branches dry up, break,
and the trunk cracks, caves in. Slowly consumed by everything. Or the confinement can end from without: e.g., by
giving the tree freedom, an excess of space, light, air, water,
nourishment, by which it's made to unfold in a series of
ecstatic flowerings, abruptly followed by exhaustion, withering. At last the tree dries up, a mute block that is slowly
consumed by itself. By everything.

It was a question of an escape from reality. The problem that should have been solved was solved, instead of the
problem that should have been solved in the first place, and
so on.

I sang in the mild evening air instead of writing a note
for my novel about how in this place I might possibly sing
in the mild evening air.

Everything in order to buy time.

As usual, I wished to sneak up on life, see how it was,
and then make up my mind about whether I would live or
not.

After we'd just been married, on our wedding night, I
sneaked through the gallery to the bathroom in order to see
him and make a decision.

When he went out, I sneaked down into the enclosed
courtyard in the colonnade to see what he took with him, if
he brought an umbrella and suitcase, a hat, glasses, gloves,
card, cigarettes, maps, newspapers, flowers, chocolate,

wine, boxes of underwear, perfume, if he took the car or not, and if he looked extroverted or introverted.

Or I sneaked from the enclosed courtyard into the garden in order to look through the hedges to see which way he drove, or perhaps walked, or ran, and if he looked back.

Or sneaked over to the window in the evening when he came home to see if he was alone.

Or sneaked over to the chair near the kitchen door to listen to him using the phone. Sneaked back and forth outside his door while he worked. Sneaked in and looked at him from behind and from the side. Sneaked into his wardrobe to see his face when he picked out his clothes. Sneaked in to see him looking at himself in the mirror. Sneaked in to sneak into his bed to see him get up. Lay and listened. Dozed. Heard him sneaking around. On the stone steps, on the terrace, by the door, on the tiled floor, in the drawing room, in room after room, in the dining room, in the living room, in the sitting room, in the garden room, in the salon, in the tea salon, the smoking salon, the literary salon, in the library and back again, in the salons, in the rooms, on the tiled floor. I heard the way he opened one of the umbrellas and let it twirl through his fingers, as he loved to do when he talked to the cat. The cat, by the way, that he once scolded for knocking over the large bouquet of multicolored tulips that he himself had just knocked over with the umbrella while he spoke about the imagery of certain artists, about water and water lilies, parasols and white clouds and fabrics, a wealth of the kind of luminous tangible things that are supposed to evoke the intangible and which now had suddenly assembled in one specific place in the world, resting around me like a bell, while I lay and listened to his sneaky steps. Dozing.

I could clearly hear that someone was coming. On the stone steps. It was she. On the terrace. Near the door. On the tiled floor. She had her own key. She was already standing near the door to the drawing room. And now, moving through room after room. The dining room, living room, sitting room. And so she was already in the garden room before he ever got past the tiled floor at the foot of the stairs. He hurried through room after room. She, in the salon. He, in the dining room. She, in the tea salon. He, in the drawing room, sitting room. She, in the smoking salon. He, in the garden room. She, in the literary salon. He, in the salon. She, in the library and back again. He, in the tea salon, smoking salon, she, in the literary salon, smoking salon, he and she in the tea salon, he and she, he and she no longer sneaked anymore, but danced together, ran, in fact, laughing, through the salon, the garden room, the sitting room, the drawing room, talking, through the dining room, on the tiled floor, on the stairs, through the gallery, the wardrobe, past the mirror in his bedroom where the key was turned. I sneaked back and forth outside the door until at last they got tired and fell asleep

After that I sneaked around as though in a daze. It was a question of gentleness, by which I, with great determination, tried to decide whether he should have his freedom or a more insidious poison.

One day while I was dozing under the wide rhubarb leaves I looked from the garden through the hedge to the street and suddenly saw her over there sneaking back and forth, and I felt like a diver who finds himself at the bottom of the ocean one minute and on solid ground the next, unable to hear whether the others are saying he's alive or dead, the air was so thick and warm and green and poisonous, because she had surely already discovered me and, with the greatest silence, sprayed her poison at me, a poison that quickly stripped all the leaf-flesh off my body, exposing my ribs, fluids, and reproductive system, causing me to cave in, collapse, crumble, almost vanish; yes, there was actually only a little dust remaining under the wide rhubarb leaves when I got up and sneaked into the house in order to buy more time.

At last, one evening, he sat in the kitchen at the large table with the red-checked cloth waiting for his meal.

I took out a salad left over from the previous day. The greens had turned brown at the edges and had yellowish spots and creases, and the tomatoes were exceptionally pale.

I opened a can of asparagus and a can of shrimp, drained the liquid, and added them to the salad.

Then I stood there awhile tossing it as if in a daze.

I chopped an onion, more tomatoes, and a couple of hard-boiled eggs, whose whites were blue or violet or almost black, and threw everything into the salad bowl.

The original salad was now nearly hidden. I gave it a little toss, spread out my arms, and almost laughed.

I then took out another bowl, made of ceramic and glazed in two shades of brown that flowed into each other in a speckled pattern. I poured in plenty of oil, shook in a good amount of wine vinegar, sprinkled in some salt and pepper, and crushed a couple of garlic cloves.

Then I took the bowl in my arms, stirring and continuing the motion, as if dancing, across the wide floor.

I snipped a head of lettuce into strips, letting them fall into the dressing with some of the chopped, hollow stems of the spotted hemlock, water hemlock, and the fine-toothed leaves of the rank lettuce opium, whose milky exudate quickly blended with the dressing. I poured the contents of the first bowl over the top and mixed it all together. And, as usual, I placed it with bread and wine on the red-checked cloth on the large kitchen table where he sat waiting for his meal.

Even after I had rolled down the window and sung in the mild evening air, I couldn't remember if I buried him under the wide rhubarb leaves, under the tiles near the fountain, under the sandstone sculpture, or if I placed him stiff and upright in one of the hollow columns in the colonnade in the enclosed courtyard, or lay him just as stiffly but horizontally in one of the many carved wooden chests along the wall of the gallery, for example, the one with the telephone under the picture of the composer who continuously stared at the black spot on the whitewash where I stubbed out my cigarette while he listened to his own music. And dozed.

When I finally reached Louise, she sat there completely still, a mute block that was about to consume itself slowly. She was clearly pregnant.

The floor and walls of the hospital room were covered with yellow and blue tiles and, because of their intricate pattern, they shimmered with a greenish tint, a color intensified by the light entering the room, which wasn't direct sunlight but reflections from the apple orchard outside. There was a vase with a couple of tulips next to the bed. I had just bought a large bouquet of multicolored tulips at the entrance to the hospital grounds, but when Louise acted as though she didn't see me, I put them down on the floor and sat on a wooden stool back by the door and stared at the picture hanging on the whitewashed portion of the wall over the tiles, and at the little black button that was used to call the staff. Katarina was sitting on the bed trying to get Louise to answer a variety of simple questions, but she was keeping her silence and her blank stare. Now and then I looked at Katarina from the side and after she lifted her arms a couple of times and her dress tightened, I became more and more certain that she was also pregnant.

Finally, Katarina got Louise to talk about mountain passes. They talked for a long time going back and forth about whether Passo S. Gottardo was 2109 or 2111, Sustenpass 2224 or 2222, Oberalppass 2044 or 2045 or 2046, and Passo del Lucomagno 1917, 1918, or 1919. Numbers and passes continued to buzz peacefully around a long line of place names—Tessin, Lugano, Bellinzona—Biasca, Lugano, Bellinzona—Lucerne, Zug, Biasca—Lucerne, Como, Chiasso—Chiasso, Biasca, Zug—Tessin, Biasca, Chiasso—making Louise more open and warm, but at the same time, tiring her out, for she suddenly said:

—She killed him.

They both looked at me, and Louise said pointblank:

—You've killed him.

Then she jumped up and began tearing at my clothes and hitting my face. I shoved her onto the bed and pressed the black button, and while Katarina and two nurses in blue who'd come hurrying in held her down, I thought about how it was all beginning to go badly for the novel I was writing, which was in my suitcase, its finished and unfinished sections, with a layer in between consisting of extra bras, girdles, panties, stockings, sandals, scarves, gloves, creams, cosmetics, and a white hat, all rolled up in a glossy transparent plastic tube with a handle made of twisted gold thread.

*

I began to long for Sampel to come home.

I always called him by his last name. Sampel, I said, Sampel, Sampel, with shifting tones, and in this way it became familiar, going from a name that belonged to everybody to something that belonged only to me, especially in our intimate moments, when I whispered, moaned, and shouted it out with joy; he was delighted to hear it in this way.

Conversely, he called me Bet, never anything else; no one who knew me called me anything else—Bet, they said, Bet, after they had heard him call me that only once, Bet, although my name is actually Bathsheba.

I thought I looked very much like that famous woman, a bit disheveled, a bit tired, stout, and immodest, but still curled round myself and my large stomach, shy, and loving.

I threw my kimono around me. The silk was shiny. Yes, I actually looked like her more than ever now that my period had stopped, my skin alternately pale and flushed, my eyes shone with fatigue or glimmered with hope, and my stomach swelled up and weighed on my attention.

I longed for Sampel to come home so I could tell him that I was going to have a baby.

Consequently, every morning I took everything out: bras, girdle, underwear, stockings, sandals, scarf, blouses and dresses made of artificial fabric—colorful and shiny, or pale and flat, a few in gray, black, or white—an array of gloves to go with them, and a white hat in case I happened to be in the garden or on the terrace when he came.

I took off my kimono and went over to the window. The plants spread out over my shoulders like an extension

of my hair. There was nothing to see. I mean, no one to see.
No one to hear. The lake was deep and shining, just as the
sky was deep and shining. And the mountains on the other
side were reflected across the entire lake so that there was
no place for the sky to reflect, at least not from this vantage
point; the mountains were deep and shining.

I turned around and saw how they were reflected in the
mirror over my dressing table, so that I, with this deep and
shining background could sit and look into my own deep
and shining eyes. I sat down and moved my hands around
the many creams and cosmetics. I opened a couple of jars
and closed them again. Most of them had screw caps, and
they were almost all used up. One bottle had a greasy ribbon around its neck. I fiddled a bit with most of them, put
some perfume on the back of one hand and some lotion on
the other, used gobs of cream on my breasts and began to
paint my mouth, first cyclamen, then beige, then scarlet,
and then rubbed it all off. Then I brushed my hair, combed
it behind my ears, and saw that I had made a middle part,
a kind of perfect symmetry with the mountains as background. I found a bra and put it on; it would soon be too
small. And a pair of light green silk pants with three small
lace flowers and a slit on the left side. They had gradually
become a couple of sizes too small. And looked ridiculous.
Bathsheba with clothes on. Then I carefully painted my
mouth again with my newest lipstick so that it looked like
a dried, pitted, but also soaked, whitish apricot, and I
painted my eyes as well with their nearer and more distant
features, so that at last when I looked into them, they
seemed to be quite deep and shining against the background
of the mountains that were also deep and shining.

Then I threw my bathrobe around me again and went

into the kitchen where I made the usual pot of tea and two pieces of white bread with raspberry jam and placed them on the heavy tea cart, which was so heavy it really needed two people to push it from the kitchen to the sunroom where several times a day I had tea, first in the morning after pushing in the tea cart, something I attached a great deal of importance to even though I was alone. And yes, I was mostly alone.

The squeaking casters always summoned the dog, and he would begin to chew on the raised threshold as soon as I opened the door.

In order to get him to move I gave him a cookie from the plate on the writing desk, and he immediately ran in and sat in the big blue armchair.

I smiled at him as I pushed the tea cart over the raised threshold trying not to let the lid bounce off the teapot and the tea to spill over and wet the napkins or the bread, and it almost always dripped over the edge of the plate and down onto the cart's shiny tiles, cutting off in places the floating blue-mountain pattern where it would otherwise be impossible for the eye to stop its own fall, ascent, flight.

I sat in the chair across from the dog and began to drink my tea.

At the bottom of the cup I saw my eye.

It didn't seem to be my eye, but a more beautiful eye . . .

I really looked into my eye. Looking from down there into my eye. And longed.

Longed to speak with someone. Confide in someone. Surrender myself. Look into another's eyes. Sampel, Sampel. The shifting tones.

Sampel gave me the dog so that I wouldn't be alone when he had to travel. As now.

When presenting the dog, he immediately named him Goethe, and everyone who met him also called him Goethe. Including me, if I called him anything at all. For, although he couldn't talk, there reigned a painful silence between us.

By the way, Sampel, with much amusement, later taught him to leap up onto the blue armchair after he got a cookie from the plate on the writing desk. Then he sat there smiling—and how that dog could smile—boldly sharing his anxious awareness of the painful silence that's always a perfect calm for those who can't talk. Won't talk.

The darkest spot in the sunroom is Goethe on the blue armchair, but it is also the only dark spot. Everything else is altogether dazzling and, if there's any color, it's the same color as the tulip beds before they come into bloom, a pale green. By the way, the furniture is made of ivory. A couple of pieces are, of course, just painted white. But that's not so important. What's important is that they give off light. Shining as if in answer to the day's changing weather, which throughout the day fills the sunroom's seven tall windows: the three along the south wall that stretches the width of the house, with, by the way, Lake Walen immersed in the landscape far below; two to the west, overlooking a couple of lower-lying small houses with their gardens and trees, with paths through the grass on the steep slopes down to the dock; and one to the east, with an unobstructed view of blue mountains floating in the distance.

Finally, there's a window to the north, and it's largely because of this window to the north that the sunroom has earned its name. Because of its design, this room can catch the sunlight from the earliest to the latest hours, even on the longest and lightest summer day.

I sit here and wait.

Later in the day, Goethe brushes a fly away with his shaggy tail.

That motor I hear in the distance is not his boat anyway.

Slowly, I surrender to my longing, go to bed without turning on the lights or washing, and cry myself to sleep.

Or I don't surrender, but get up. Morning after morning I get up, look out over the lake and mountains that are deep and bright, drink tea and look at my eye looking into my eye from the bottom of the cup, listen for the boat. Let Goethe out when he needs to go, maybe go out myself, or sit for hours looking at the shiny tiles of the tea cart, the floating blue mountains, the rugged ravines in the dark blue glaze, the forests, the rivers, waterfall, and the miners with their oblong barracks that dripped a bit during the firing, just like the decorative tourists, one of them always with an arm gracefully lifted: Look! They're so small you can't even see their eyes.

I sit here and wait. If, previously, I said the sunroom earned its name, well that's no longer true. What I said about the dazzling light from early until late as recently as yesterday may have come from a memory of the architect's vision, which he must have had one cold winter's day when Lake Walen was covered with snow. With ice and snow.

First of all, the house is nestled into the high, almost completely vertical mountain range that follows the unbroken range on Lake Walen's north side and casts a deep shadow.

Second, the mountainside directly west of the house has a large, protruding, and very threatening rock outcrop that blocks the light from the early afternoon, and casts a shadow.

The third thing is that the mountain to the east is so high that no matter what the circumstances, it's a good long time after sunrise before light falls onto Lake Walen. And it casts a shadow.

But what really makes the sunroom so dark, particularly in the summer, are the three towering plane trees on the south side of the house where the sunlight otherwise could enter the three tall windows unobstructed; however, if the truth as stated in this account is to come close to the actual circumstances, the trees cast shadows into the sunroom in three solid blocks, rather than there being simply light, sunlight.

In this way I confronted my longing.

Or I gave it its freedom, an excess of space, light, air, water, nourishment, causing it to unfold in a series of ecstatic flowerings, abruptly followed by exhaustion, withering. At last, the longing stopped, a mute block, slowly consumed by itself, by everything.

The fullest flowering happened one day at around noon in Sampel's rose garden. The air was warm, thick, and green, and raised the dust as though it were tears, salt crystals and skin the same consistency as pulverized lava, dry and soft.

I walked between the tall hedges and bushes with their walls, columns, and portals, their stairs, towers, slopes, and ravines, with the bushes' underground prison cells of roses. Rosa rugosa, Rosa rubiginosa, Rosa pimpinellifolia, cream-colored Rosa "Nevada," yellow Rosa hugonis, and deep scarlet Rosa moyesii. I drifted as if in a desert, from coverlet to coverlet, from cloud to cloud, becoming a diffuse, shimmering part of the mirage that cut my eyes with its invisible grains of sand. Its heavy fertilizing pollen.

Sampel's rose garden. His passion. His eccentricity, as

someone called it. He designed and planted it himself. He researched, fertilized, cultivated, and cataloged it, knew all the names and made up his own pet names, which he mumbled to himself, or inadvertently to me, and always with shifting tones.

He has said, with a smile, that the rose garden was designed for seduction. And in a string of novels he's described the seduction of a string of women in a rose garden like this. But no one has ever seen him enter it with anyone, neither man nor woman. Nor have we been here together. He comes alone. And I have permission to come here alone. As now.

In the wide middle section the roses were lower, tighter, and flower after flower burst in a swarm of soundless explosions, mute outbursts. There were so many that when you tried to follow a particular rose's movement and then looked away for a second, it instantly became confused with another, and in this way it seemed you could see them opening, suspended in the air for a moment, motionless, and then drooping, falling, shriveling up. They lay there in a multicolored heap, and you could see them turning into dust, you could smell them dying, dry and soft.

I lay a whole day among the petals allowing my longing to wither. Gradually it stopped, a mute block consumed by itself, by everything. When I again went up toward the house at night, the air was clear and unscented; I turned on the terrace light and glanced back at the rose garden. At that moment I understood that I had always talked about the rose garden's character, but now for the first time I could talk about the rose garden itself, its continuous destruction.

A couple of days later, when summer began to get darker, although never completely dark, I suddenly began to call myself Bathsheba, and did so particularly when I noticed that I was starting to show. I gave Goethe a friendly smile and, on top of that, broke the painful silence: Goethe, I said in shifting tones, Goethe. But I took it further and began to actually examine the dark sunroom. I turned on the light, never bothering to roll the heavy teacart in, but having my tea in different places in the room, luring Goethe away from the big blue armchair simply with a cookie from the plate that was now moved from the writing desk. Goethe, I said, Goethe, and he immediately sat down at my feet and let me scratch him behind the ear, or he put his paws on my lap and looked at me, a little affectionately, a little sorrowfully. I opened the windows and breathed in the mild evening air. One of the windows facing west, however, was so overgrown that it wouldn't budge. It was so green that it was darkened, was covered by leaves, was sealed from the outside by Virginia creeper and ivy with pale climbing feet that you could just make out on the pane like birds stuck to it, barely visible on the pane behind the climbing roses' vigorous flowers and leaves on a tightly coiled wire frame stretching up from a hole in the floor where the roots of the plants were buried. Stretching up and bouncing like toy clowns on springs and covering the window on the inside almost more completely than it was covered on the outside, so that it was more difficult to make out the glued bird feet from the inside. It's been said that a woman once threw herself out of this window, without completely killing herself, however. After that Sampel, in all likelihood, with his own hands, planted the climbing rose, this vigorous plant that he, with his own hand, described in one of his books more or less the way I've just cited from memory.

The climbing rose actually died a long time ago from a lack of light, water, and nourishment. All that remained was a stiff skeleton. Most of the leaves were pierced by thorns and rustled in the draft from the open windows. Others were diminished and gray; a few still had a little leaf- green under the thick dust. A fat light green caterpillar was in the process of eating its way through the last bud. The aphids had devoured the rest and were now twitching stickily, caught in their own satiation. I cut up the entire plant into small pieces, then swept them together and took them out. I left the root alone and the next day hired a man to make some yellow and blue tiles to fit the hole, matching the colors and pattern of the worn tiled floor as best as possible.

After that was taken care of and the room was made tidy and clean, I once again got down to work on this novel. Both the finished and unfinished parts with their related used and unused notes have been sitting on the writing desk among the letters, clippings, and papers since that morning when I first began to suspect that I was pregnant.

At first my new situation made me want to give up the whole project, yes, I actually found it altogether preposterous to think of Sampel's relationship to other women now that our own relationship had such a strong significance.

But gradually, as time passed, now that I was in my sixth month, with Sampel still traveling, and since I was unable to track down where he was staying, I felt forced to return to my original plan of writing a novel in order to reach him, which, from the beginning, had been my plan, namely, to write a novel in which I present Sampel to the women I know he's known.

So he would know that I knew that he's known them.

So he would find out when he came back.

Or if he doesn't come, he'd know when the book came out.

Of course, my story, for good reason, couldn't be as realistic as it would be under Sampel's direction. Yes, I was not the one present. That's what it was all about. I've been outside events that were actually about me. Therefore I must write them down. And they'll always be recognizable to those who have actually experienced them.

I got this idea while reading Sampel's latest novel.

As early as page eight I noticed a very incisive and loving account of the woman Azorno, the main character, meets.

At first I was flattered to think that Sampel had used me as a model for this compelling description, but gradually, as I read on, it became clear that he was describing someone else.

I then made a string of inquiries that resulted in five possible candidates. I couldn't immediately make out which of them was the woman from page eight, and therefore made up my mind to write a novel in which I would present Sampel to the four ladies he knew so well and, undoubtedly, he also knew their names: Randi, Katarina, Louise, and Xenia.

And I counted on this recognition, counted on him recognizing them, knowing them better, understanding them better, and explaining to me that these women were absolutely not the way I had written about them. My only chance of tracking down the right one depended on my ability to read Sampel's reactions.

At the same time that I was working out the different women's accounts, I felt, however, an increasing longing for this Azorno, a longing that clearly made the stories different from the way I first thought of them, but they have also culminated independently, apart from the way I conceived them during my stay in the rose garden where, while dozing in the noon heat, I was lying there mumbling his name, Azorno, I said, Azorno, and the rose petals surrounded me like the sky, so that within a second I was swept back ten years in time, and I think I felt like a diver who finds himself at the bottom of the ocean one minute and on solid ground the next, unable to hear whether the others are saying he's alive or dead because he's encapsulated in a silence as vast as if he'd brought the ocean up with him and it surrounded him now like a huge bell that no one can pass through without drowning.

This experience gradually began to take up a large part of my consciousness as I continued to work on the novel, and the upshot was that I thought more about Azorno than Sampel.

Suddenly one morning, after these recent developments at my writing desk, I had an intense feeling of being so much a part of what I had written that it was impossible to go further unless I got to know the others involved.

I had a difficult time finding Xenia's address because it apparently hadn't yet made it to its final place in Sampel's card file where the other three names were written down with several old addresses crossed out. I invited them, lured them down here with the help of four identical telegrams: Randi. I'm longing for you. Come. Sampel; Katarina. I'm longing for you. Come. Sampel; Louise. I'm longing for you. Come. Sampel; Xenia. I'm longing for you. Come. Sampel. If they come I will present them with this novel, and hopefully in this way force them to reveal if they knew, had known Azorno, or if it was only Sampel they were interested in. Little by little I began to feel strong enough for such a confrontation. If they came. If they come.

I've made up the two guest rooms, Sampel's bedroom on the other side of the wardrobe and the mirror, and my own bedroom with the fluttering plant curtains. I'll sleep in the sunroom, which I've already decorated with large bouquets from Sampel's rose garden. On the hearth I've made a symmetrical arrangement with two glass pitchers of a pink spray of Queen Elizabeth and Betty Uprichard. On the tables around the large, blue armchair I've gathered the yellows, Peace and Rumba, surrounded everywhere by Golden Showers that lavishly, almost to the point of excess, fall from the tabletop toward the Rosa hugonis and Rosa pimpinellifolia in crocks on the tiled floor, so that together in a really beautiful combination they make a dazzling yellow sea in the middle of the sunroom. The writing desk is covered with Blaze Superior and Rosa "Nevada." Finally, as a way of underscoring the ingenuity of the arrangements, I've placed a single white rose, Virgo, in the window facing north, precisely the window that should've earned the sunroom its name.

I've opened the windows to let in the mild evening air.

Goethe plods around quietly and now and then sits down decoratively under the Rosa hugonis like a genuine porcelain dog.

The novel is laid out. The light is turned on. I sit and wait. The next morning when I carry in my tea and two pieces of white bread with raspberry jam on the small tray, which I've now begun to use again when I'm alone, I hear the boat down on the lake already. The crossing takes only five or six minutes; it's the walk up the steep path from the dock to the house that takes time.

As soon as the boat begins its return trip, I know that if the passengers are heading up here, they'll soon swing round the last house by the dock and begin the ascent.

I go over to the window. The ferry, a small motorboat that's the area's only connection with the outside world, is already halfway across the lake, and then, my goodness, there really is a woman turning onto the path and slowly moving toward the house. She's rather tall and dressed in a white coat, white hat, and possibly also white gloves. When she gets a little farther up where the wind is stronger she has to hold her hat with one hand, and when a gust of wind suddenly throws open her coat, you see that under it she's wearing a dress with large flowers, but in particular that she loses her umbrella, which, unfortunately, rolls off the slope of the cliff, and she stands there watching it for a moment. Perhaps it was blue. She stands there for a moment as though on stage, giving the impression with her movements that she's enjoying the view and the blue sky that nonetheless makes the umbrella superfluous, and that she thinks she's being watched. By Sampel.

I carry out the small white tray and when I hear her opening the door to the garden wall, I go down to unlock the door.

She surprises me with her youth and her very long, very light hair.

—Is Sampel here? she asks.

—He's unfortunately not home. What else could I say?

—Do you know when he'll be home?

—No, I really don't know.

—I thought he was supposed to be here now.

—I couldn't say, but would you like to wait?

—Yes, thank you.

She's very friendly.

I take her white coat, hat, and light hand luggage, offer her tea or coffee—she chooses tea—and lead her up to the sunroom where I ask her to sit down.

—There must be a lot to do in a big house like this, she says when she notices the roses.

—Yes, there certainly is, I say.

When the tea is ready and I roll in the teacart with different kinds of bread, cheese, and jams, I hear the boat out on the lake again.

—Is Sampel coming after all? she asks when she sees that there are two teacups.

—No, not just now, I say. I'm not expecting him.

And it's clear that, until I sit down and begin to drink tea with her, she thought that I was some kind of domestic help.

—Oh, are you his secretary? she says, glancing over at the novel on the writing desk.

—Yes, I say, in fact I am. And his wife.

I realize only then that she's pregnant. She returns my glance. Perhaps we're both wondering who's furthest along.

—I completely forgot to introduce myself, she says.

It was Xenia.

We sat for a little while in silence. Ate. It was a silence that I considered breaking with an explanation before it became painful.

—I think someone's coming, she said.

I also heard the door in the garden wall open and shut behind someone now moving with quick strides across the gravel path and then the terrace.

I went down and unlocked the door.

—Good afternoon, said a very large woman in a pair

of wrinkled pants and a loose-fitting dark blue sweater, clearly showing her advanced pregnancy.

—Good afternoon, I said. May I take your bag? It was a gray canvas bag that she preferred to keep with her.

—Has he been waiting long? she asked on our way up. Obviously no one could imagine that Sampel was married, although they must have all surely known; but certainly not that he was married to me, this obviously none of them could or would imagine.

—No, he isn't home, I said.

—I thought so, she said, and as we stepped into the sunroom: My goodness, it's Sampel's rose garden.

—Oh, good afternoon. I almost thought you were a flower, she said to Xenia. I didn't see you; they're the same shade of yellow.

The flowers on Xenia's dress and the Rosa hugonis were the same yellow.

—Yes, I think they are, said Xenia.

They introduced themselves. It was Randi.

She preferred coffee, and I went out to fill her request, speculating about whether I should explain the situation now or wait to see if the other two showed up.

—I hope you'll excuse me, said Randi when I returned. And when I looked confused she added: For not introducing myself.

They had obviously talked.

—But I actually didn't expect you to be here; well, we can speak candidly, I thought he wanted to see me because of this.

She pointed to her stomach.

—No, he isn't home, I said and regretted immediately that I didn't say at that moment that I'd invited them.

—No, I understand that, said Xenia.

—He hasn't been home since before I found out that we're going to have a baby, I said before I could stop myself.

Randi mumbled something. Then we sat in silence for a while. Ate. And furtively measured one another's stomachs. As though the important thing was to be first.

When these assessments and silences, interrupted by a few absentminded exchanges about roses, had lasted for some time, and after I had finished preparing a little speech with my inner voice about the purpose of my invitation, I heard the boat.

—Isn't that the boat? Randi said.

—Yes, it does sound like the boat, Xenia said.

—It's the only connection to the outside world, I said.

With that, all three of us got up and went over to the window.

The boat docked. And a woman came walking up toward the house. By now the people in the little houses near the dock had something to talk about. We, on the other hand, were silent, listening to the boat's motor starting, following it with our eyes across the lake. For that matter, they were also certainly talking in the houses on the other side of the lake—the little houses next to the other dock. The boat reached the other side, and the woman now had a good part of the cliff path behind her so that we could see she was rather short and heavy and dressed in a black coat that must have been far too warm now that the sun was at its peak. When she had nearly reached the top we heard the boat's motor starting again over on the other side.

—This is certainly becoming a real gathering, Randi said.

I was already on my way down to unlock the door.

It was Louise.

She had on a gray dress with a white lace collar and white cuffs at the wrists. She looked neat and childlike, though she was clearly one of those women who as a child grows up all at once without fear and immediately takes on an intense, calm, sometimes haggard or doomed expression that never really leaves. It was clear that she had changed her style because of the pregnancy.

When we came upstairs to the others she said:

—Is this the sunroom that I've heard so much about?

—Yes, isn't it wonderful with all these roses? Xenia said.

I asked if she'd like tea or coffee. She said she'd like a cup of tea.

—You might as well make a whole pot, Randi said. Actually, another woman is coming up the path.

Katarina was also on her way.

As I waited for the water to boil, I at last reached a decision that would have unfortunate consequences.

Now that I knew of their condition and had every right to suspect that Sampel was behind it, and when none of them suspected me of being behind the arrangement of this gathering, I made up my mind to let them believe that Sampel with his uncontrollable longing had lured them here in order to show them that their longing was more uncontrollable than his.

I counted on there being a kind of unspoken connection between us that would cause them to react positively to my proposal to spend a couple of days holiday with me. Eventually I would admit that I felt so alone.

After they had begun to settle down, if the conversation flagged and the silence became painful again, I would read them the novel. Of course, only I could see that the finished part was a poor representation of the actual situation, but there was still a possibility that the others involved would have another perspective that I could then take up and work into the unfinished section. In this way my objective to have a confrontation between the book's five women would certainly be attained.

I heard the door in the garden wall open and went to unlock the door to the terrace.

It was Katarina.

She had on a crumpled whitish hat and a sporty blue jacket that couldn't be buttoned over her large stomach. Her orange corduroy jumper was also beginning to tighten and the little white blouse that she had on under it was rather dingy.

I pretended not to notice, whereupon she, with great perceptiveness, immediately looked as though she were excusing her appearance, and said:

—Sampel wanted to see me?

—Well, I said, unfortunately he isn't home, but may I offer you a cup of tea? It's ready and I'm sure you could use one, right?

—Yes, thank you, she said, if it isn't any trouble.

—No, it isn't at all, I said. I've already made it. I should tell you that I've unexpectedly received a visit from a couple of ladies this morning, well, actually, you're the fourth, but one more or less is just lovely.

She didn't appear to be in complete agreement, but followed me anyway up to the sunroom where the tea party, now complete, would find its final form.

We chatted a little about the house's setting, the grand view was mentioned, we chatted about the deep shining lake and the deep shining mountains, about the trip down here—they'd been on the same airplane—and about the trip out here—they hadn't all been lucky with the transportation from Zurich—and about the small boat, about the houses down by the dock whose inhabitants now had something to talk about behind the curtains, and about the steep path up the cliff that led to the house, about the house itself, still one more time about the house's wonderful setting, and finally a long, incisive, lavish, almost excessive chat about the roses, which inevitably led us to the essential, Sampel.

Then Xenia said with a little bitterness:

—Isn't it wonderful that your husband can afford to live so beautifully and have such a beautiful wife as his beautiful secretary here by this beautiful lake in beautiful Switzerland where he can cultivate his beautiful rose garden in peace.

But Randi immediately took the initiative to turn the conversation in another direction:

—I'm used to speaking directly and I'll do so now. Since we all know the truth, we might as well say it out loud: Sampel simply has gotten all five of us pregnant. And not only that: he would like to make it clear to each of us that he has put none of us in an exceptional situation. Why else would we be sitting here staring at one another's stomachs? I therefore suggest that we properly remove our rotund selves in a peaceful manner and leave the scene to Sampel's wife. In any case he's not going to hear anything more from my child and me. She patted her stomach. Not a word.

Xenia, Louise, and Katarina already looked solemnly resolved and began digging in their handbags with their cigarettes and gloves, looking at the clock, and, presumably, trying to figure out flight connections.

I seized them in their confusion and spontaneously presented my long-prepared invitation.

—I have an idea, ladies; now that the damage is done, would you like to be my guests for a couple of days? I suggest that we simply relax and try to find topics of conversation other than that persistent Sampel.

Of course, I was thinking about the novel.

After some polite protestations they all allowed themselves to be persuaded and installed in the rooms already made up for them.

I now began to delight over the fact that I, who had been absent at the events all this time, was now driven to action, or rather, had thrown myself into a series of actions that would give me a voice, or maybe even give me power over those involved, including myself.

The lunch and plentiful wine softened us and made us full in tone like large, round gourd instruments. The air and light played over us as we moved down through Sampel's rose garden where we passed the afternoon in company with our bodies' wonderful melodies. The tall hedges and bushes with their walls, columns, and portals, their stairs, towers, vertical dives, and columns, with the bushes' underground prison cells of roses that opened with our laughter, and without really talking we conveyed to one another a delight that had the same quality as freedom: an excess of space, light, air, water, nourishment, whereby we could make ourselves unfold in a series of ecstatic flowerings—maybe it was this effect that Sampel was thinking of when he said that the rose garden was designed to seduce—but it would always be abruptly followed by exhaustion, withering. Eventually we stopped, mute blocks slowly consumed by themselves. By everything.

I think it was this experience that sank into us as we settled in the wide middle section of the garden, dozing, chatting, knitting baby clothes, and playing with Goethe, who'd been let out after being confined during the arrivals of the morning.

After a rather late dinner we gathered once more in the sunroom for coffee. The fragrance of the roses was strong. We opened the windows and breathed in the mild evening air. The sun was about to go down somewhere far behind the mountains; the final blush from the clouds in the sky rested on our scarlet, beige, cyclamen, rose, and apricot-colored lips that moved gently around cups, cigarettes, offering a few words now and then, perhaps confidences.

I had gone from being an increasingly indistinguishable part of what I had written, to a position outside of it, listening, watching, executing.

It was almost dark now. The lights in the little houses down by the dock were lit, and from time to time we could follow a pair of headlight beams over the cliffs on the other side of the lake. Goethe walked around, letting us scratch him behind the ear.

When we couldn't see each other anymore I turned on the lamp on the writing desk, and before we had a chance to start talking, as people always do when there's suddenly light, perhaps to defend themselves against unfamiliar glances, I told them that I was writing a novel and that I'd like to read the finished section to them.

I took out the manuscript. We adjusted ourselves. But just as I was about to begin I heard the boat.

—Isn't that the boat? Xenia said.

—Maybe more people are coming, said Louise smiling.

—Now it doesn't matter, said Katarina.

We decided it was probably a guest of someone in one of the houses down by the dock, and I began reading, but the whole time I read I heard the boat, heard the motor idle and then press on again, heard it working the whole way on its return trip, that familiar sound that finally ebbs away, dies out. I read. A short time later Goethe suddenly sprang up and ran over to the door. Then we heard steps, the door to the garden was opened and shut, I didn't read any more; we heard someone unlocking the door to the terrace.

—It's him, I said.

—Sampel, they said, as though with one mouth.

We all got up and stood there, completely still.

When Sampel walked in I went over and turned on the overhead light.

Before he could say anything, Randi jumped on him. Xenia was the next to attack. It was unclear whether Louise and Katarina were also attacking Sampel or trying to stop Randi and Xenia in their attack, and, for that matter, it was unclear what I was doing, for the fight was now in full swing.

We lay in a colorful heap on the floor with roses and broken pieces of vases and crockery over and under us. Goethe barked and ran back and forth anxiously, or tore at our clothes with his sharp teeth. At some point he licked my eyes with his large rough tongue and I was terrified that he would lap them up. I kept on grabbing scarves, bags, and the contents of purses—makeup, paper, and cigarettes—which had pressed out between the bodies. I kept on grabbing silk fabrics that were wet and full of broken glass and the roses that had scratched all of the fighters' arms and legs. I think I looked for Sampel. I think I wanted to free him. But my hands found only the swollen bellies and enormous hanging breasts, some of them bare, scratched by nails, teeth, rose thorns, and broken vases. For a second I thought I saw down into his eye as though down into a cup. I think I tried to free him. But I kept on grabbing bras, girdles, underpants, stockings, sandals, scarves, dresses, and skirts of artificial fabric, colorful and shiny, or pale and dull, and with them a number of gloves, a white hat. And the roses, roses, roses.

Suddenly everything stood still.

Suddenly I was completely alone.

Before me on the floor lay Sampel. Blood poured from two large gashes at his throat and temple. He was dead.

Randi, Katarina, Louise, and Xenia had gone without my realizing that they had left.

Peace and Rumba, Golden Showers, Queen Elizabeth and Betty Uprichard, Rosa hugonis, Rosa pimpinellifolia, Blaze Superior, Virgo and Rosa Rugosa, Rosa rubiginosa, Rosa "Nevada." This continuous destruction.

Now I sit here and wait . . . Sampel's prisoner, here where darkness spreads with the speed of light.

*

Whenever I write a novel I live in Rome, Via Napoli 3, tel. 484.409–471.565.

Sampel, at present, Rome, Via Napoli 3, I write at the top of each and every sheet of paper, including, as a rule, the telephone number: 484.409–471.565.

It's a habit I have from when I wrote letters just as often and as painstakingly as you wash your hands. Several times a day.

Several times a day I wash my hands in this way. But I

don't write letters. No one knows this address. No one should know it. No one should know where I am. No one knows.

Not even the employees at the hotel know. I registered myself as Azorno in the guest book so that they would take me for one of their own. Someone anonymous, a loafer, a dreamer who does hard seasonal work in order to have the freedom to loaf and dream.

Little do they know that I rest by loafing and dreaming in order to do the hard seasonal work here in their very own hotel.

Several times a day, first thing in the morning, I write on one sheet of paper after another: Sampel, at present, Rome, Via Napoli 3.

It's a street that leaves me in peace. I can eat and sleep in peace. I can distract myself watching my neighbors in peace. And I can work on this novel. In peace. Everything is in the most perfect order. I have escaped here precisely to be left in peace.

Everything is thus in the most perfect order: the bed, the dark wardrobe with the mirror, the bedside table with the vase—where, by the way, on another occasion, I placed a couple of tulips—the wash basin, the shelf with the toothbrush cup, pills, and razor, the wine-red armchair, the wastebasket and the chair by the desk, the desk. The most perfect order: ashtray, cigarettes, paper, and some fruit. The curtains are dark green, heavy, and faded. The walls are whitewashed. Every spring they're whitewashed. I'm glad that the curtains can be closed. And I'm glad that the walls don't have wallpaper or pictures.

I am glad, however, that the walls have one picture. Once I absentmindedly stubbed out my cigarette against the wall so there's a black mark on the white chalk. It's of course been whitewashed over, but a shadow of it is still faintly visible. The little cigarette mark on the whitewash is right by an old portrait, or, more precisely, right by the nose of an unknown man in profile, who was drawn on the white paper with such a thin and black line, then framed and hung on the wall over my desk. I call him the composer. His kind expression is directly aimed at the mark. Every time I write a novel I hang him up in that place so I can comfortably forget myself looking at that always kind man, the composer, his eyes, his mouth. I listen to his music. I never get tired of it. Several times a day, first thing in the morning, I let him hear the description of the window facing north, where I once planted quite a wonderful climbing rose. A wonderful music.

After preparing him with the day's theme, I go down and drink my coffee with the others from the street. I don't look at them because they aren't to think that I want to look at them. Most of the time there's an old floor rag I can look at. It twitches on the tiled floor, licking the yellow and blue until the floor becomes shiny and appetizing.

I usually get another cup of coffee so they can see that I'm not looking at them.

When the floor rag isn't there I usually pick at an old sandstone sculpture, a little greenish manikin with over-sized ears and waves down the chest as on a washboard to signify frizzy hair. It sits on a shelf in a niche that is painted blue. I have picked a little hole in his right thigh without anyone seeing me. And all the while I think about what I should write on this or that sheet of paper, which in the morning I had inscribed with my name, first my name: Sampel, at present, Rome, Via Napoli 3, and then a description of the window facing north where I once planted that wonderful climbing rose.

The window's so green that it is darkened, is covered by leaves, is sealed from the outside by Virginia creeper and ivy with pale climbing feet that you can just make out on the pane like birds stuck to it, barely visible on the pane behind the climbing rose's vigorous flowers and leaves on the tightly coiled wire frame stretching up from a hole in the floor where the roots of the plant are buried. Stretching up and bouncing like toy clowns on springs, and covering the window on the inside almost more completely than it is covered on the outside so that it is more difficult to make out the glued bird feet from the inside. It is said that a woman once threw herself out of this window, without completely killing herself, however. After that I planted the climbing rose with my own hands, that vigorous plant I've written about with my own hand in one of my books.

Thus I escaped here in order to write about this for the composer every morning after writing my name at the top of the paper: Sampel, at present, Rome, Via Napoli 3.

Then I drink coffee while looking at the floor rag and the little sandstone sculpture.

Then I climb up from the bar, buy grapes at the usual stand, and take them up to my room.

Then I close the window and look at the woman in the room across the way.

When she's finished washing herself and dressing behind the door of the wardrobe so that I can't see her, and has left the room, and when I see her leave the building, I sit down at the desk with the day's sheets of paper.

I now see that the climbing rose died a long time ago from a lack of light, air, water, and nourishment. All that remains is a stiff skeleton. Most of the leaves have been pierced by thorns and rustle in the draft from the open windows. Others are diminished and gray; a few still have a little leaf-green under the thick dust. A fat, light green caterpillar is in the process of eating its way through the last bud. The aphids have devoured the rest and are now twitching stickily, caught in their own satiation. After a series of ecstatic flowerings, it suddenly became exhausted, withered. Which I will explain.

First I will work out a general explanation.

Then I will explain everything to Xenia.

Then I will explain everything to Randi in general terms.

Then I will explain everything to Katarina, and in particular, my escape.

Then I will explain everything in general to myself, and in particular, my escape to Rome, Via Napoli 3.

Will then explain to myself.

Explain myself.

Explain

Plain

In

In the late afternoon at five o'clock I go out again.

If I haven't already gone out at twelve o'clock or three o'clock.

Or I don't go out at five o'clock, not until nine o'clock in the evening. I sit hiding at the edge of the large circular fountain that, splashing, catches all of the jets of water used for rinsing off the women and swans placed in their calculated positions in the middle of the Piazza della Repubblica after having been carved in stone. I hide in the dense row of people occupying the edge of the fountain. This dense human row is part of the dense human mass occupying the entire square that is in motion like a necklace on the earth's bosom being hit by beams of light, rays, in flashes, glinting like lightning, a few women in white hats, men in white shirts against dark skin.

How much have I told them? I drag my fingers through the lukewarm water thinking about how much I've told each person, how much I've told some and not the others, how much I've told one and not the others, and how much each one has then told the others and not me, how much they've told one another and not me.

Perhaps they all know that the climbing rose was in no way withered. On the contrary, just when the flowering was at its peak, I cut up the entire plant into small pieces, then swept them together, and took them out. I left the root alone, and the next day hired a man to make some yellow and blue tiles to fit the hole, matching the colors and pattern of the worn tiled floor as closely as possible. At the same time I ordered a fountain, which I would set up later so that it would splash with a tone other than rain.

After I'd confessed that the climbing rose was in no way withered, and after I'd seen the woman who dresses behind the door of the wardrobe walk by, I decide to slip unseen from the dense row of people at the edge of the fountain and sneak back to my room where I will immediately write that the climbing rose was in no way withered.

Or I don't go out at nine o'clock in the evening or at five or three o'clock in the afternoon, but only in the morning and, therefore, without seeing my neighbor get up and get dressed. I don't see her in a white hat between the cars in the Piazza della Repubblica in the evening either. Still, I confess, and as soon as I come home I write, that the climbing rose was in no way withered, and then I go to bed with the scent of the warm mass of people still clinging to my body.

This mass of people . . .

The women.

Whenever I write a novel I make plans for a rose garden for the women, designed to seduce. I research, plant, fertilize, cultivate, and catalog it.

I want to see them moving freely between the hedges and bushes, between the walls, columns, and portals, on the stairs, in towers, or resting in the bushes' underground prison cells of roses. Rosa rugosa, Rosa rubiginosa, Rosa pimpinellifolia, cream-colored Rosa "Nevada," yellow Rosa hugonis, and deep-scarlet Rosa moyesii. They will drift as if in a desert, from coverlet to coverlet, from cloud to cloud, becoming a diffuse, shimmering part of the mirage that will cut their eyes with its invisible grains of sand. Its heavy fertilizing pollen.

In the wide middle section the roses will be lower, tighter, and flower after flower will burst in a swarm of soundless explosions, mute outbursts. There are so many that when you try to follow a particular woman's movement and then look away for a second, she instantly becomes confused with another, and in this way it seems you can see them opening, suspended in the air for a moment, motionless, and then drooping, falling, shriveling up. They lie there in a multicolored heap, and you can see them turning into dust, you can smell them dying, dry and soft.

Or I first go out at night, after I've written about the roses all day. I get out of bed and get dressed without turning on the light. Over on the table lie the sheets of paper ready for the next morning: Sampel, at present, Rome, Via Napoli 3, tel. 484.409–471.565.

This mass of people . . .

The women.

A few of whom are still strolling in the streets.

Every morning I write at the top of the page: Sampel, at present, Rome, Via Napoli 3, and go out. After I've had coffee in the downstairs bar and watched the woman across the way get dressed behind the door of the wardrobe and go out, I sit down to work on this novel I've started, and then go out again at five or three o'clock in the afternoon, nine o'clock in the evening, or late, late in the evening in the warm streets when only a few of the mass of people are left, after I've written about the roses, the rose garden designed to seduce, and about the women who move in a completely perfect order, although never com-pletely perfect, since they may be seen lying among the petals throughout a whole day allowing their longing to wither. Gradually they stop, mute blocks consumed by themselves. By everything.

Or I go out at twelve o'clock, noon. When she's finished washing herself and dressing behind the door of the wardrobe so that I can't see her, and has left the building, I sit down at the table with the day's sheets of paper to begin work on this novel. I look at my name: Sampel, at present, Rome, Via Napoli 3, and at the picture, which I hang in this place every time I write a novel so that I can comfortably forget myself and look only at that always kind man, the composer, his eyes, his mouth. Listen to his music. I never get tired of it. Several times a day, first thing in the morning, I let him hear the description of the window facing north: The climbing rose was in no way withered. Just when the flowering was at its peak, I cut up the entire plant into small pieces, then swept them together and took them out.

Or I get up and follow her through the warm streets, hiding in the evening in the middle of the Piazza della

Repubblica where from my place at the edge of the fountain I see her go by in a white hat and white gloves against her dark skin against the dark evening. It's been said that a woman once threw herself out.

Or I first go out late in the evening after I've slept with the scent of the warm mass of people still clinging to my skin. After I have worked on this novel the whole day. I never get tired of it. Several times a day, first thing in the morning, I let him hear the description of the window facing north: The climbing rose was in no way withered. Just when the flowering was at its peak, I cut up the entire plant into small pieces, then swept them together and carried them out. It's been said that a woman once threw herself out. I returned that time to my desk. She had really thrown herself out. The window was open, and I was compelled to breathe in the mild evening air.

Or I go out only in the morning and don't return the whole day. After I have slept with the woman in the room across the way and watched her get up and wash herself and get dressed, not as she usually does behind the door of the wardrobe, but right in front of the bed so I can see her, and after she has left the room. And the building. I go out and drink coffee while watching the floor rag and the little sandstone sculpture. Bet, I say, Bet.

Then I climb up from the bar, buy grapes at the usual stand, and take them up to my room.

Or, as already mentioned, I go out only in the morning and don't return.

*

While I wrote this novel I visited Sampel every day.

—Everything is in the most perfect order, he said: The

bed, the dark wardrobe with the mirror, the bedside table with the vase—where, by the way, there are a couple of tulips that I brought with me—the wash basin, the shelf with the toothbrush cup, that wine-red armchair, the wastebasket and the chair by the desk, the desk. The most perfect order: ashtray, cigarettes, paper, and some fruit. The curtains are dark green, heavy, and faded. The walls were whitewashed. Every spring they're whitewashed.

—I'm glad that the curtains can be closed, he said.

—And I'm glad that the walls don't have wallpaper or pictures, he said.

The floor and walls of the hospital room, the walls, up to where the whitewash began, were covered with yellow and blue tiles and, because of their intricate pattern, they shimmered with a greenish tint, a color intensified by the light entering the room, which wasn't direct sunlight, but reflections from the apple orchard outside.

—Xenia, come and see, isn't your name Xenia? You have to see the roses, he said with a friendliness so clear and extroverted that it verged on self-surrender.

—It's designed to seduce, you know.

And then he chanted his eternal rose formula: Rosa rugosa, Rosa rubiginosa, Rosa pimpinellifolia, cream-colored Rosa "Nevada," yellow Rosa hugonis, and deep-scarlet Rosa moyesii.

—Their sisters, he said, their sisters are designed to seduce. These rose sisters. And then he laughed.

—There are so many that when you try to follow a particular woman's movement and then look away for a second she instantly becomes confused with another, and in this way it seems you can see them opening, suspended in the air for a moment, motionless, and then drooping, falling, shriveling up. They lie there in a multicolored heap, and you can see them turning into dust, you can smell them dying, dry and soft. I lose myself in this slide of roses, these sisters I plan, cultivate, and catalog. These sisters in jealousy. Yes, you need to know the names, he said, and it's best to have a couple of pet names as well. I use pet names, especially when I'm working with hybrids. They should not have real names until just before they're full-grown. Then, of course, they should definitely have them.

I was afraid he would start up again with his rose formula and so I began talking about the picture hanging over his desk. It was a very simple pen drawing that was a clear depiction of Sampel in profile.

—It must be you, I said.

—Yes, I made it myself. Can you see the little mark on the paper?

—Yes, what about it?

—Right by his nose, he said, that's what I made first. I stubbed out a cigarette on the paper, without burning it of course. It's supposed to be a rose. And next to it I drew myself.

—Why did you write Azorno at the bottom? I asked.

—Azorno, that's me. I call him the composer. His kind expression is aimed directly at the mark. It's a self-portrait.

When I wasn't visiting Sampel, I was in Tivoli writing this novel. I made careful observations of the soundless fountain, of the fountains in general, their splashes, the pale green of the tulip bed, and the gardener's vision, the big trees to the right of the main entrance, and in the evening, the dense mass of people, the white shirts, white hats.

During the day, my attention was especially drawn to

individual women. Women with baby carriages, women in the rain with open umbrellas, red, blue, green, or women in the sun with white hats . . . one woman dozing during the noon hour, while in her thoughts picking a small hole in a rock that was partially hidden between the bushes.

I always tried to tell Sampel about my experiences in Tivoli and about the work with the novel, but as a rule I found him lost in his beautiful rose garden, sitting by the window, researching and cataloging, unable to tear himself away from the complicated rose formulas. Or he sat dozing, allowing the words to mumble on their own: Rosa rugosa, Rosa rubiginosa, and so on. Then he would suddenly get up and go over to the window and count the colors outside: cyclamen, beige, scarlet, pink, apricot, yellow, and cream.

—It's completely green, I said. The green grass, the green leaves, the branches, bushes, trees, the green sap.

—Yes, it's green, he said, thick and warm and green and poisonous, because they have already discovered me, and, with the greatest silence, sprayed their poison in through the window, a green poison that quickly strips all the leaf-flesh off my body, exposing my ribs, fluids, and reproductive system, causing me to cave in, collapse, crumble, almost vanish; yes, there's actually only a little dust remaining and that can be easily brushed off the sheet before lying down, as if there were a little sand between the toes the evening before. Room for the next one.

—Sampel, I said.

—Yes, he said suddenly, though he never used to answer to that name. Yes, I did kill Bet.

—Bet is not dead, I said. You only remember that because you've described it in one of your novels.

—I remember it perfectly, he said. It was the day I drove

too far west of Passo S. Gottardo 2109. I drove due east, up over Sustenpass 2224, but when I finally approached the Gotthard area, I was confused by the views and ravines, the bridges and tunnels, glaciers and streams, the commemorative markers for generals apparently of Russian descent, by the cows on the roads, by the flowers called alpine flora among the stones, and in Andermatt, by the police officers, to such a degree that I drove across Oberalppass 2044 instead of across Passo S. Gottardo 2109, and had to continue down through Tschamut and Sedrun with the headwaters of the Rhine far below me; it was here that I threw her out the window, I know it, why else would I remember these names so clearly, and why else would I remember how I reached the slightly larger town of Disentis / Mustér, 1133, where I stopped to ask directions and was told I had to turn due south and drive up over Passo del Lucomagno 1917, which I then did, so at last at Biasca 293 I found the road that would've taken me much more quickly over Passo S. Gottardo 2109, Biasca 293, where the lush Tessin valley with its river and vineyards began to stretch down toward Bellinzona 241, with a scent of Italy beginning, approaching via Lugano 334, and fully present in the hot, crisp, spicy landscape around the border at Chiasso and Como 201. And now, as you can see, I'm in Rome.

—No, you're here, I said, shaking him.

—Sampel, at present, Rome, Via Napoli 3, he said, tel: 484.409–471.565.

It was after such outbursts, when I sat looking at Sampel's portrait of the composer, that I understood it was a question of a confinement. Azorno was trapped inside Sampel, in Sampel's beautiful rose garden, in the bushes' underground prison cells of roses designed to seduce. There he sat by the window among the blue and yellow tiles with the greenish glow from the apple orchard outside, dreaming, while he continuously researched, cultivated, and cataloged. When he had made the last hybrids, and when, after going through an endless row of pet names, he arrived at the correct names, then Azorno would come forth like a composer and play his wonderful melodies on the women's bodies. He dreamed.

In Tivoli the broad tulip beds had long since bloomed according to the vision of the gardener. They had already started to bend and stretch in all directions. Many people were standing still in the sun admiring them or strolling around the lake, which wasn't blue but had the same mostly pale green color of the tulip beds before they bloomed. Or they stood before the silent fountain loudly making comments. On rainy days I could sit in peace writing my novel. One woman with a wet and crumpled white hat sat down next to me at my table but didn't disturb me. One woman with a cat in her bag took it out and showed it to her companion when the waiter turned his back. Several women were strolling around with their umbrellas open, there was an abandoned baby carriage by the fountain. The opened umbrellas were red, blue, or green. One woman with a red umbrella sat down at a table and ordered two Camparis. She pulled the table toward her so that her feet and legs all the way up to her thighs and crotch were hidden under the round tabletop, and sat with a straight back and open umbrella and paid the waiter as soon as he brought the two Camparis under the red sky. The rain buzzed around her. Almost considerately. She drank one of the Camparis, then held up the little lemon slice against the gray sky. She ate it. Drank the second Campari and got right up. I have seen her play this scene so often: the red umbrella, the two Camparis, or the green umbrella, and the two martinis. Always the same. Getting up right after and leaving Tivoli.

It was a question of a confinement. And after that the problem can be solved in two ways: Poison or freedom. Both equally gently. Every confinement can be terminated from within: e.g., by giving the tree poison and quickly paralyzing the tissues in their different functions; when everything stands still in this way, a mute block, all movement begins to go downward: flowers disintegrate, leaves curl up, rustle, are carried away, twigs on branches dry up, break, and the trunk cracks, caves in. Slowly consumed by everything. Or the confinement can end from without: e.g., by giving the tree freedom, an excess of space, light, air, water, nourishment, by which it's made to unfold in a series of ecstatic flowerings, abruptly followed by exhaustion, withering. At last the tree dries up, a mute block that is slowly consumed by itself. By everything. But to solve something for others that you cannot solve for yourself demands that first and foremost you refrain from using these two means of solving the problem. It could seem that life, even with an excess of freedom and beauty, has only one message: this continuous destruction, outside of which we are forced to choose to stand, as a kind of extension, where we can function without understanding what it's all about. To solve something for others therefore means that instead of solving the problem that should really be solved, you might accidentally solve another problem. Strictly speaking, it is no longer a question of a problem, but the conditions. There is nothing to be solved, but something to bind. Bind one to the other. Bind yourself to a random person whose random circumstances cause you to no longer recognize yourself simply as a human being, but rather as a human-made being.

These were the kinds of experiences that sank into me, especially on rainy days when I sat in Tivoli and the rain buzzed around me, almost considerately, as the fountain splashed with a tone other than rain.

The next time I visited Sampel, he was sitting as usual by the window with the view to the apple orchard, mumbling his rose formulas.

—Everything is in the most perfect order, he said. The bed—I sat down on the bed—the dark wardrobe with the mirror, the bedside table with the vase where the tulips now bent and stretched in all directions, the wash basin, the shelf with the toothbrush cup, the wine-red armchair—he was sitting in the wine-red armchair—the wastebasket and the chair by the desk, the desk. The most perfect order: all these wonderful hybrids, he said, Rosa Biasca, Rosa Bellinzona, Rosa Chiasso and Como, Rosa Lugano, all of these wonderful hybrids that cannot be crossed with Rosa rugosa, Rosa rubiginosa, Rosa pimpinellifolia, cream-colored Rosa "Nevada," yellow Rosa Hugonis, and deep-scarlet Rosa moyesii, then at last I reach my long-planned pet names, these improved rose sisters, Rosa Katarina, Rosa Randifolia, Rosa Louise and Rosa . . . what's your name?

—Xenia, I said.

—Rosa Xenia, he said.

It was a question of gentleness.

—Rosa Xenia, Rosa Xenia, he said with shifting tones, as if he were searching for a particular tone of voice. He just continued repeating it: Rosa Xenia, Rosa Xenia, and sat down next to me and began to caress me, saying it continuously and in increasingly entangled figures, saying it while we took off our clothes, unceasingly, and now with even clearer harmonies, he continued to say it—while we made love—like a station that at last fades. Azorno, I said, Azorno. The shifting tones.

It was a question of gentleness.

Afterward he lay there, still humming with his mouth close to my right ear, carefully turning my nipple around like he was adjusting a radio dial, while I picked a little at the sheet under his head and ran my fingertips around and around the folds of his left ear. We listened, watched, and reacted to things at the same time, as indistinguishable parts of the music. The continuous music.

After we had gotten dressed we decided to push the little black button that was on the whitewashed part of the wall under the picture of the composer. We asked the two nurses in blue who'd come hurrying in about Sampel's medical record; however, we had to wait several days, weeks, for it, and all the while we, almost considerately, tried to keep the music in our ears that had a tone other than the rain that buzzed against the windowpane and farther out against the apple orchard's green leaves.

When we at last got it, Azorno read all about Sampel.

It grew into a very long and actually a very sad story, which I'm completely incapable of retelling, mainly because I object to the record's way of presenting it. It didn't speak about Sampel (and nothing at all about Azorno), but about his character.

By the end, however, the story held the promise that we should meet in Tivoli just to the right of the main entrance, under those big trees where the people waiting don't get in anyone's way. I was wearing a white hat, and when I passed through the turnstile everything fell completely silent.

The man waiting for me was really Azorno.

Within a second my blood, thoughts, nerves, and senses were swept back ten years and I felt like a diver who finds himself at the bottom of the ocean one minute and on solid ground the next, unable to hear whether the others are saying he's alive or dead because he's encapsulated in a silence as vast as if he'd brought the ocean up with him and it surrounded me now like a huge bell, and Azorno came whirling into it, without drowning, grabbed me in his rush and swung me around, laughing. Then we walked on into the gardens with our arms around each other.

The big trees' shadows slid peacefully over and past us while Azorno spoke about the imagery of certain artists, about water and water lilies, parasols and white clouds and fabrics, a wealth of the kind of luminous, tangible things that are supposed to evoke the intangible, and which now had suddenly assembled in one specific place in the world, resting around us like a bell, Azorno said, a silence.

*

As soon as we got down here I set to work on inscribing my sheets of paper: Azorno, at present, Paris 6e, Rue Dauphine 52, so that if they got lost they could easily be returned to me.

Bathsheba teased me, saying that I shouldn't believe that anyone would consider that a piece of ordinary white paper—which, to boot, probably wouldn't be very white by the time it was found—could have any value at all simply because it had a random name and a random observation or experience written on it; did I really think that someone would consider sending random information about a fountain that splashed with a tone other than rain back to me?

Nonetheless, when she had unpacked and set up the room, she helped inscribe the sheets of paper.

On the trip down they had been in one of her suitcases: at the bottom the finished sections of the novel with related used and unused notes, and on top of that a multicolored heap of extra bras, girdles, panties, stockings, sandals, scarves, gloves, creams, cosmetics, and a white hat, all rolled up in a glossy transparent plastic tube with a handle made of twisted gold thread. In a little mesh bag, two blouses and one dress were crumpled together and yet, even in this condition, they were ready to use because they were made of artificial fabric. I'd filled the holes and spaces in between with writing pads of different sizes, until I more or less had a flat surface five centimeters under the lid of the suitcase. On this flat part I put the unfinished sections of the novel with related used and unused notes.

And so we started the car and drove slowly into the city from its most outlying neighborhoods where the rain had stopped and the trees shone in the headlights, making our way onto broader and longer roads, where the rain had stopped and the asphalt shone in the headlights, and finally we let ourselves be pulled with the current into the city, where the rain . . . where the city lights were on.

The city glided by and settled behind our car that glided on and adjusted itself to the road that was now completely straight and sang in the mild evening air. Houses glided by, but mostly flat wide fields glided by, transforming themselves far out in the semidarkness into distant cities and eventually into mountains where the rain had presumably also stopped and the invisible shone in the headlights. We rolled the window down and sang in the mild evening air.

We've made this trip so often, at different times of the day and night and in different weather, but still, regardless of the actual circumstances, I always return to exactly that description, as though gripped by language, as though it set a limit on my freedom to experience, as though when a personal expression has taken shape it reveals that that expression has its own life and actually takes shape without my help, or intervention. Almost as if it were impersonal. Something I ultimately don't have power over, maybe not even a say in the matter.

After we inscribed all the sheets of paper and had taken over the room, we divided it into zones according to function and need: the bed and nightstand, with the vase that Bathsheba had already put a bouquet of tulips in, were for sleeping, being together, and inner maintenance; and the washbasin, the shelf with toothbrush cup, etc., and the wardrobe with the mirror were for outer maintenance; finally, we reserved the wine-red armchair for Bathsheba to read the newspaper in; and with the opposite corner, the wastepaper basket, the chair by the desk, and the desk itself, was for writing the novel. We left the walls and curtains as they were, white and green. The only thing we moved was a little black porcelain dog that was on the windowsill and at last we found a place for it on top of the wardrobe, because it mustn't fall out when we opened the window, which is exactly what we did now that everything was in the most perfect order. Later we called it Goethe because of the deep expression of its shiny eyes.

—The air is unusually mild this evening, I said.

—Shouldn't you make a note of it? Bathsheba asked,

although she knew very well that I would later write that we sang in the mild evening air.

I kissed her.

And it was a question of gentleness.

When we had been there for a few days we began, as usual, to alternate between going out together and alone. Bathsheba went back to the shops that we'd lingered outside of and bought scarves, hats, and a single light blue umbrella that was perhaps more like a parasol. I spent most of my time in the Luxembourg Gardens, where I took most of my notes. I especially studied the area with the fountain, the tall jets of water that rose in the middle of the basin and the people who continuously moved around it or stopped or sat down to watch it, just as I sat and watched it. Or they watched one another. We watched one another. In the farthest corner of the gardens, on the other side of the tulip beds where the gardens looks more like an open meadow with grass and mostly plane and chestnut trees, I found, in the shadow of the large canopy and of the smaller trees that were spread around, an old greenish sandstone sculpture, a little manikin with oversized ears and waves down the chest as on a washboard to signify frizzy hair. When I looked closer I realized that he had fallen down from a pedestal that was completely covered with leaves from the small trees, and the back of it it was also covered with Virginia creeper and ivy with pale climbing feet that you could just make out. I bent the branches back and tore away the tough ivy in order to get to the inscription, but first I had to remove the remains of a climbing rose that was close to the stone and had long since withered from a lack of light, air, water, and nourishment. All that remained was a stiff skeleton. Most of the leaves had been pierced by thorns. Others were diminished and gray; a few still had a little leaf-green under the thick dust. A fat, light green caterpillar was in the process of eating its way through the last bud. The aphids had devoured the rest and were now twitching stickily, caught in their own satiation. I pulled it away from the stone, but there wasn't much left of the inscription. Name and date were illegible, and I could decipher only that it was about a composer.

Despite the fact that I could certainly make many similar finds in that more intimate part of the gardens, I always returned to the fountain and circled around it. I was particularly absorbed by its endless splashing, babbling, and described it in this way over and over again, the jet of water rose in the middle of the circular basin, rose up as through a plant stem that has long been thirsty, or rose like a resistant glass tube sent vertically into the air from the glassblower's mouth, or rose and fell like green plants' green hair, their long hair, like long hair in a completely free fall down through space, although never completely freely, always a little sticky, like hair that clings to the skin, that clings to the body, that clings to blood, that rises, rose, and falls, fell, or splashed, babbled, settling on its source and mumbling over and over the first words it has learned.

It was these words that were babbled and mumbled in a language I didn't know or understand; there was a drowsiness in the language that time after time made me believe that behind my back, somewhere in the garden there was a person who at exactly this moment made exactly these notes to be worked into a novel about me, while I made them to be worked into my novel about Sampel.

One might think that the language, unaffected by anything, continued its own life, even in its most elaborate expression, and in spite of continued attempts to prevent it from encroaching on the freedom to experience.

Whenever I had those kinds of notes with me from the gardens it was always a great comfort to be with Bathsheba, just wandering around in the streets, sitting in a cafe drinking wine, chatting about different things, and now and then breaking off a piece of bread on the red-checked cloth and eating it while we waited for the salad. Or buying grapes at the usual stand, taking them up to our room, me kissing Bathsheba, licking her eyelashes with my long rough tongue, spitting the mix of garish colors onto the white walls, terrified that I'd lap up her eyes, while Goethe sat smiling from the top of the wardrobe.

Or at last we'd go for a long walk in the Luxembourg Gardens.

Bathsheba would go out early so that I could have some peace to organize my notes and perhaps prepare myself to take new ones during my walk in the gardens.

It was, of course, clear to me that there always exists an intimate relationship between an author and his main character, but if it turned out that we continued on as identical, indistinguishable parts of the same language, I would consider the possibility of taking on the role of my own narrator in my own novel, and thus see any future notes from a more unconditional point of view.

After putting the situation in order, or, more correctly, after a moment of considering the actual situation as the truth, I cleaned up after myself, my cigarettes and bathrobe, newspapers, a book. Then went out.

It was the first Sunday in May and the noon hour was unbelievably hot.

We were supposed to meet just to the right of the

entrance, under those big trees where people wait so they won't get in anyone's way. She had on a white hat and had opened her blue parasol so that I'd be able to spot her.

Within a second my blood, thoughts, nerves, and senses were swept back ten years and we whirled toward each other and the big trees' shadows peacefully slid over, past us, and I heard myself speaking about the imagery of certain artists, about water and water lilies, parasols and white clouds and fabrics, a wealth of the kind of luminous, tangible things that are supposed to evoke the intangible and which now suddenly had assembled in one specific place in the world, resting around us like a bell, I said to her, a silence.

By this time we had come to the wide tulip beds. All the tulips were the same pale green, but the groupings had faint suggestions of other colors as well, and I understood that they would bloom in a specific pattern according to the vision of the gardener, a vision he must have had one cold winter's day when the Luxembourg Gardens were covered in snow.

While she chatted about the flowers and the weather, I began to tell her about my new novel, but she calmly continued to speak about the way the tulips were growing and was about to mention a bouquet of multicolored tulips she once received, when we sat down at a table and ordered two Dubonnets. She pulled the table all the way in toward her so that it touched her stomach and she sat with a straight back and open parasol, and smiled at me when I paid the waiter as soon as he brought the two Dubonnets under our blue sky. I took her hand, and while I played with it a little awkwardly, maybe with a slightly studied awkwardness, I revealed to her that she, exactly as she was sitting there, was the woman whom the main character in my novel first meets on page eight.

—Are you sure? she said teasingly. Close your eyes and tell me what I have on.

I closed my eyes and began with the blue parasol. Then the white coat, white hat, and white gloves.

—And when the wind blows your coat open, I can see your large-flowered dress.

She laughed. And when I looked at her again, she closed the parasol, took off her white hat, and said that I've known her long enough to realize that it's not dreams that come true.

—Yes, I said, I've known you for ten years.

She actually had on an orange sleeveless dress made of a thin fabric that hung loosely on her and moved with every little puff of wind. Her dark coat hung over the chair because it had become hot now that the sun was at its peak.

—And you still believe that I continue to pupate in a white coat, which you conjure with your endless string of pet names.

—What's wrong with them? I asked.

—Or you believe that I go around in a pair of wrinkled pants and a loose-fitting dark blue sweater so that you can ironically call me Grandiflora.

—I've never used that name, I said, or at least I don't use it anymore.

—Or I have on a little gray dress with a white lace collar and white cuffs, so that you can call me Bet. Bet, you say, Bet.

—But you've had a dress like that, I said.

—Yes, and a white coat.

—And I stopped calling you Bet a long time ago, I said.

—Yes, you don't call me that anymore, but deep down you still believe that I am, or I have been, will be, your own little Bet.

—But, I said.

—No, she said, I know what you're going to say, there's nothing wrong with pet names, and there isn't, but it can be, it can become a role, assigned or chosen, or both at once, and without knowing how it actually happened you're suddenly stripped of your freedom to experience or be experienced.

She said this calmly, looking calmly at me. Her eyes were deep and shining, and the sun shone on her light hair, which was parted in the middle and combed behind her ears. She surprised me again and again with her unbelievable youth, although she was clearly a woman who as a child grew up all at once without fear and immediately took on an intense, calm, sometimes haggard or doomed expression that never really left. As though she had once and for all made up with life, had bound herself to me, bound herself to a random person whose random circumstances determined that she could no longer consider herself simply as a human being, but rather as a human-made being.

—Bathsheba, I said.

—It doesn't really matter whom you're married to, she said.

—Yes, I said, you're right, and because of this we can no longer consider it an accident that we live together.

—I had actually wanted to say something completely different, she said, but of course they're related: We're going to have a baby.

I put my arms around her shoulders and kissed her. It was a question of gentleness. We walked silently around the gardens and watched the many people moving together or alone in the excess of light and air. We stayed in the gardens until evening. She looked wonderful without a hat or gloves. With the dark orange dress against her dark skin against the dark evening. Only her teeth shone when she opened her mouth, only the whites of her eyes if she didn't lower them, and her nails faintly on her dark ungloved hands.

We sat at the edge of the large circular fountain that, splashing, caught all the jets of water. We hid in the dense row of people occupying the edge of the fountain. This dense human row was part of the dense human mass occupying the entire area. We hid ourselves in the scent of the warm mass of people whose scent also clung to our bodies.

This mass of people.

I was thinking that this was my only life.

It is my

only life.

I scanned it so there was an emphasis on "my." Perhaps to invoke my feeling of possession.

At the same time it was clear to me that behind my back somewhere in the gardens there would be a person who just at this moment was thinking that this was his only life.

It is my

only life.

A person. Maybe more. Who just now thought exactly this.

When the gardens were about to close and the water jets sank down so that the water's surface became calm, there was a moment of soundlessness, everything was silent, though certainly never completely silent, since there was the sound of many people's movements quickly increasing, as the sound of all that I have written was quickly increasing and limiting my freedom to experience, but it was in this moment of soundlessness that we got up, and the whole time I heard Bathsheba breathing, and I kissed her, it was in that moment that we kissed each other, that for the first time in our lives we experienced the mild evening air. And sang.

When the sea heaves and is rough, the seething waves in their turbulence form pictures resembling creatures; it seems as if it were these creatures that set the waves in motion, and yet it is, conversely, the swelling waves that form them. Thus, Don Juan is a picture that is continually coming into view but does not attain form and consistency, an individual who is continually being formed but is never finished, about whose history one cannot learn except by listening to the noise of the waves.

—Søren Kierkegaard